The Art of Mindful Facilitation

By Lee Mun Wah

Cover Design by Lee Mun Wah
Press by Nitu Rai, Krishna Copy
Editing by John Lenssen
Production by Keri Northcott

ISBN: 978-1-4507-7016-3

A Prelude

Whenever I am asked what the art of mindful facilitation is all about, I am reminded of the simple words of the Dali Lama, "Life as a free and fortunate human being is precious because it gives us the opportunity to cultivate the awakened mind." To become awakened, we need to be truly alive to what is happening around us; to notice what lies before us and in the moment. The clues are all around us, in the words that are spoken, in the silences that deafen a room, to a simple downward glance in the middle of a conversation. We have only to notice and to listen and to respond.

So much of my family experiences and Buddhist teachings have helped me to notice the world around me. For example, early in my life I learned of the interdependence of all things and events; that I was never alone in my actions. What I did affected all those around me, reflecting upon my family, my relationships, my community, and even my destiny. All of these concepts and ways of living and relating are foreign to the Western experience, which is often focused on the individual and not the community, on profits and not on relationships, on the future and not on the past.

When I was growing up no one ever asked me how I felt as the only Chinese boy in my classes or my thoughts coming from an Asian perspective. Nothing in my education valued or saw the history of my people as relevant or useful in this American culture, except our foods and New Year celebrations. My silence was mistaken for passiveness, my accent for ignorance. What was missed were the very best parts of my family and myself – our enduring sense of tradition, our scientific and literary contributions, our spirituality and our deep connections to our ancestors. My roots are from a land of empresses and emperors, warriors and philosophers, poets and actors, painters and scholars. But that was never mentioned in all my years of schooling. You see, my assimilation into this culture was to begin where they wanted me to be, not from where I was. I wanted someone to ask me how I felt as a Chinese person and what I needed. In retrospect, what happened to me was not assimilation, but rather, accommodation. An accommodation to a predominantly Eurocentric perspective.

To me, that is what the art of mindful facilitation is all about - helping others to become mindful of our interactions with one another by noticing our connections and disconnections, as well as the impact of our words and actions. In learning what makes each of us who we are, we can choose to transform that knowledge into compassion and understanding. And through our compassion and understanding, we gain a deeper respect for and honoring of each other's journey and contribution.

Lee Mun Wah

Acknowledgements

There are many to whom I am deeply indebted for their help with this book, through their inspiration, support and knowledge. I particularly want to thank John Lenssen, who volunteered to help edit this book and whose kindness and wisdom I have long admired. In knowing him as a teacher and friend, I have become a better person.

I also want to thank the many cast members from my various diversity films - Stolen Ground, The Color of Fear, and Last Chance for Eden - who paved the way for me into living rooms and boardrooms across this country. Their stories and courage opened the hearts and minds of people everywhere. They gave words to the pain we have all long felt, but which had not been heard. Each of them are my models of integrity and compassion. They are truly heroes.

A special acknowledgement for my dear friend Monty Hunter, who helped me begin my career as a director, supported me through countless fundraisers, was one of the key camera persons on The Color of Fear, and who helped me choose the film crew. His selflessness and kindness will always be appreciated.

I would also like to thank my mentors – Harrison Simms, Ricky Shirover-Marcusa, Gary Hoeber, Robert Chope, Phillip Hart, Frank Mar, Tom Chinn, Robert F. Kennedy, Mahatma Ghandi, Nelson Mandela, and Thich Nhat Hahn. Their kindness, charity, and wisdom transformed me and inspired me to help others.

Finally, I'd liked to thank the men from my Asian & Multicultural Men's Groups, who taught me how to love myself as a Chinese man and who afforded me the opportunity to develop my life's work as a community therapist. They were the inspiration for my first film, Stolen Ground, and eventually for The Color of Fear. They were my brothers and teachers, and are the foundation for the work I do today.

A very special thanks goes to my dear friends and colleagues – Rainbow Markell, Linda Compton, David Lee, Laureen Green, Dawn Tso, Larry Lee, Reanne Young, Elaina Lovejoy, Spencer Brewer, Esther Seigel, Aliah Mahon, Lori Hill, Jennifer Myers, Seifu Haile, Melaku Girma, Heward Jue, Candice Kollar, Abbie Gibor, Lyla Diaz, Sandye Cottman, Marina Shusterman, Kathleen Butler, Kim Ina, Cassie Kushel, Rhonda Cervantes, Carlo Cervantes, Satsuki Ina, Roberto Almanzan, Simma Lieberman, Dennard Clendenin, Mei-Ling, Linda Van De Wall, Shaynah, Deven, Kalani, Henry Bourgeois, Patty Redeker, Barbara Imhoff, and Matthew Johnson.

To my editors and comrades in crime, Richard Bock and Robert Goss Jr., without whose

To my editors and comrades in crime, Richard Bock and Robert Goss Jr., without whose skills, wit and creativity I would not have grown and dared as much as I have. I owe them a great deal for their faith in what we were doing and their willingness to trust me. They each gave many late hours and long years to many film projects and premieres, often at a cost to their families. I am proud to stand with them in honor of the many gifts that came out of our efforts together. We will always be the Three Mosquitoes, irritating and inspiring, and, on rare occasions, both.

These acknowledgements would not be complete unless I thanked all the children whom I have taught for over twenty-five years as a Resource Specialist Teacher in the San Francisco Unified School District. They gave me so many gifts through their curiosity and desire to be happy and fulfilled. Through them I was able to give back what so many wonderful teachers had given to me as a child growing up in the flatlands of Oakland, California – a sense that I was special and had something to offer.

To my mother, I wish to thank you for changing the course of my life by giving up yours, and for impressing upon me the importance of family and of giving to others. And to my sister, Mei-Ling, whose friendship and caring gave me back a sense of family and hope, I am forever grateful. It was you who wrote in my high school yearbook, "Always follow your heart. To thy own self, be true." Thanks, sis, for always being there and for helping me with the wonderful cover to this book. You are a true artist.

And of course, to my dear son, Joaquim. I hope this book will give you a glimpse into why I was away so often, and will inspire you to follow your dreams, too. You are my finest piece of art and my sweetest gift in life. Someday, it is my hope that my films and writings will make this a better place for you and all the children of this world.

May you always remember to give to those less fortunate and to leap as often as you can, dancing along the edge...

Contents

Training Vignettes 40

Diversity Exercises 117

StirFry Seminars Services & Products 137

The Art of Mindful Facilitation

Facilitation is an art in the finest sense – both from the perspective of an artist and as a viewer. Each time a group interacts, a painting emerges. With careful and diligent observation, a story unfolds – enhanced or diminished by our willingness to be a bridge or an obstruction. Buddhists believe that we do not learn from our experiences, but rather by our willingness to experience.

I think that facilitation is either educationally or emotionally oriented, but seldom both. For facilitation to be truly transformative, it must come from a holistic approach – appealing to the mind, the body, and the heart. There is a saying, "Unlearning racism requires a change of heart." Real change often occurs when there is a crisis. For change to be lasting, it must move the heart enough for one to act courageously – not just in a temporary sense, but as a conscious and purposeful act over a lifetime of different relationships and situations. So a crisis can be perceived, not just as danger, but also as an opportunity for learning and for change.

I wrote *The Art of Mindful Facilitation* as a training tool for those who are interested in finding ways to create a sense of community within groups, particularly those from diverse cultures. In many ways, this book is not only about diversity issues, but also about the communication process and how to relate authentically and intimately with one another. It is perhaps a dual mirror – one to look at ourselves, and one to look at others with an open mind and an open heart. As you peruse this book, you will find that it is divided into four parts: "The Art of Mindful Facilitation," "Workshop Issues," "Training Vignettes," and "Diversity Exercises."

The first section, "The Art of Mindful Facilitation," contains important information about the techniques used in practicing mindful facilitation. One of the first steps is looking for keywords during a communication exchange. This is discussed in "Keywords" (page 5). Noticing the keywords enables the facilitator to learn about the underlying issues and needs of the participant/group. "The Art of Mindful Inquiry" (page 7) is about how to ask questions instead of making statements. Study this carefully. This is a collection of questions that will help a participant to explore more deeply how they are feeling and what they are needing. These sets of questions will also help a facilitator to better understand the underlying context to some of the issues presented by a participant/group. "The Art of Mindful Inquiry" is divided into working with the individual (page 7) and how to work with the group (page 8) simultaneously. "The Mindful Inquiry Guide" (page 9) explains the theories behind each of the questions used in the Mindful Inquiry Model, as well as some of my thoughts on how to more effectively use each question and some of the issues that might arise. One of the most common questions asked during our trainings is how to interrupt someone who is talking too long; another is to know where to stand. These questions and many others are discussed in the section entitled "Mindful Techniques" (page 17). Included in this first section are also some helpful hints and thoughts about listening and facilitating conflicts. "The Art of Listening" (page 22) was written in 1996

and has been used in counseling classes all over the country. "The Conflict Facilitation Model" (page 23) was inspired by my training and work with Conflict Resolution Boards on diversity issues. It is the model I use whenever disputes occur in my seminars. I think you will find it very useful also as a tool to offer your participants who are often inexperienced with how to deal with conflicts when they arise in their workplaces.

The second section, "Workshop Issues" (pages 25-39), contains some of the key issues that have arisen in my workshops over the past twenty-five years. I think you will find this section illuminating because it sheds some light on traditional issues from a diversity and facilitative perspective. It is my belief that the more experience we have with life issues, the more able we are as therapists and facilitators to empathize and understand our client's issues and experiences.

The third section, "Training Vignettes" (pages 40-116), reproduces actual situations that occurred in my workshops. I think you will particularly enjoy this section because it is a great training tool and also affords you an opportunity to learn the thoughts and the reasons for some of the interventions I developed. Read the "Instructional Guide" (pages 41-43) because it will explain how to use the Training Vignettes as effective teaching tools.

The last section, "Diversity Exercises" (pages 117-136) includes most of the exercises I have used in the last twenty-five years to help stimulate dialogue and model ways for groups to discuss diversity issues. Each of these exercises is illuminating and thought provoking. They were created to help promote intimacy and a sense of community awareness.

The "StirFry Seminars & Consulting section" (pages 137-146) contains a description of our services and the many films, books and diversity products that we offer. An Order Form is included at the end of the book. For more information, our website is: http://www. stirfryseminars.com.

This book is a culmination of my life's work as a diversity trainer, community therapist and filmmaker over the last twenty-five years. I have facilitated workshops and trainings in corporations, universities, government agencies, churches, and social agencies for thousands of groups throughout this country and around the world. What I have learned and witnessed fills these pages – stories of grief, sorrow, anger, hurt and despair echo throughout, but also stories about the courage and deep sense of hope that someday we will find a way to come together.

I hope that as you read and use this book, you will see it as a journey that each of us must take if we are ever to become a multicultural community where everyone is valued and represented. That is my hope and prayer – that we each become the change that we envision; that we live mindfully with each person and within each moment.

The Training Objectives of Mindful Facilitation

1. Observing what is said and what is not said.

2. Noticing the intent and impact of all communications.

3. Understanding how the impact of our life experiences can effect our attitudes and behaviors.

4. Learning how to listen and to respond effectively and compassionately.

5. Becoming aware of the effect of culture on relationships.

6. Replacing adversarial and defensive statements with mindful responses of observation and inquiry.

7. Making use of non-verbal communications.

8. Creating community within groups.

9. Experiencing and viewing anger as an intimate experience and conflict as an opportunity.

10. Beginning, through observation and inquiry, at each participant's current state of mind and level of awareness.

Listening for the BLUES

When working *with* someone:

1. Begin where they are, not where you want them to be.

2. Learn what they have gone through to get to this room.

3. Understand how their past affects who they are today.

4. Emotionally relate to how they are feeling. Nourish a relationship.

5. Stay in the room even if you are scared, or feeling angry, or hurt. Be present.

Keywords

When I am assessing what a participant is saying, I am always looking for keywords that will provide a sense of what that person needs, as well as something about who they are. These keywords are the clues to help a facilitator create an intervention that aligns with the participant's concerns. For example, if the participant says that she feels invisible, then the subtext is that she wants to feel seen. If he feels disrespected, then he wants to be respected.

It is also important to notice what is not being said. For example, if someone says that anger is no longer an issue for them because they have learned how to manage it, then the questions that might be helpful are, "What happened when you did get angry? How did it affect you? How do you compensate for it today?"

Another use of keywords is to help the facilitator establish a connection with the participant. By using his/her words, the participant feels heard and understood, thereby establishing a foundation for a trusting relationship. Too often, facilitators rush towards an intervention because of their need to "solve" a situation as quickly as possible or to stay in control.

One of the most important qualities in facilitation is the willingness to be patient – to allow the "true nature of a situation to emerge." Much like Michelangelo's sculptures, allowing the form to come forth in its own time and nature.

Underline the keyword(s) and identify what it is that each person is saying they need:

1. "I don't feel acknowledged at work. They wouldn't know what to do without me."

2. "He talks to me like I'm not there or smart enough to understand."

3. "He disrespects all the folks that aren't white. He uses a tone that just tells you he thinks you're uneducated and lazy."

4. "I'm too scared to say that I don't like being called a 'little girl.' I don't think he'd listen."

5. "All the white males who are from Eastern colleges are promoted. I've been here for over ten years and I've trained all of 'em. Yet they don't think I'm qualified enough or have anything worthwhile to say."

6. "I feel frozen when I'm in a room with all these guys."

7. "They go out to lunch with all the other managers, except me. I don't care. I have my

own friends."

8.   "They don't see how much I bring to the table. I've given up trying to be like them."

The Art of Mindful Inquiry

Processing Individual Reactions

Observational Inquiries

1. What I heard you say was…
2. What I just heard now is that you asked a question….
3. What I heard just now is that you made a request…
4. What is the statement behind your question?
5. What did you notice was the group's reaction as you were talking? Would you like to know?

Reflective Inquiries (Past/Present)

1. What's familiar about this?
2. What were you like when you first came here and what are you like now?
3. What do you leave at the door?
4. What does your company/agency lose when you can't be yourself?
5. What angered you about what happened?
6. What hurt you about what happened?
7. I was just imagining what it must have been like for you….
8. How did it affect you when it happened? How did it feel?
9. How does it affect you now? In your workplace? In your relationships?
10. How do you compensate for it so that no one knows?

Action Inquiries

1. If you could say something to_____, what would you say?
2. If you could tell_____ what you need to able to stay here, what would you say?
3. What makes it unsafe for you here and what would make it safer?

The Art of Mindful Inquiry
Processing the Group's Reaction

Observational Inquiries

1. What did you notice as _____ was talking?
2. What did he/she say? What did he/she not say?
3. I notice you had a reaction when _____ was talking.
4. What did you hear in _____'s voice?
5. What just happened here?

Reflective Inquiries (Past/Present)

1. What was your reaction when _____was talking?
2. What is familiar about all this?
3. What was hard about what happened and what was good about it? Why?
4. What moved you about what just happened? Why?
5. What isn't being said here? What's familiar about that?
6. How many of you know exactly what he/she is talking about? Why or why not?

Action Inquiries

1. How many of you want _____ to stay here? Please raise your hands. How many of you are willing to work towards some of the changes that he/she was talking about?
2. What are you willing to do today to unlearn racism at this workplace?
3. What did you learn about yourself today that will be helpful in unlearning racism? What did you learn about others today?

Mindful Facilitation Inquiry Guide
Individual Reactions

Observational Inquires: Asking questions about what you notice/hear.

1. What I heard you say was….

One of the quickest ways to connect with a participant is to use their own words. Try to be succinct. Listing too many things about what they said will not only overwhelm them, but diminish those statements that were emotionally significant to them. In other words, quality, not quantity.

Another trade secret is learning how to draw out your statements. For example, "I heard you say that you were never the same…" As an emotional response emerges, more than likely they will tell you more. Remember, your work as a facilitator is to help illuminate key places in their lives – much like an exploration for important resources, that once discovered, become useful and enriching. Have faith; the participant will tell you which way homeward.

2. What I just heard now is that you asked a question…

Many times we make statements without the benefit of hearing from those we are upset with or curious about. Sometimes because we are frustrated or angry or hurt, we postulate what we anticipate the answer might be. Often we don't always ask those involved, what their opinions are. The hard work, though, is being willing to hear the truth.

I remember a Black Bermudan man saying that this workshop was a waste of time because white men do not want to end racism because it would mean giving up their power and privileges. I then turned to him and said that it sounded like he was asking a question. I then asked him if he'd like to ask the white men in this room if what he said was true. He agreed and an incredible discussion ensued. So you see, he already knew the question. It was the answers that he hated or feared.

3. What I heard just now is that you made a request…

We often mask our desire for change inside our anguish or hurt. For example, an employee shared with the company that he was hurt that only the top white male executives went out to lunch with each other. He felt that the only time folks like himself were asked to lunch was on their birthdays, and even then, the meal was attended only by those who worked in their departments. I then turned to the audience and had them notice that he had just made a request: "I want to be asked to lunch, too."

4. What is the statement behind your question?

Many times we overlook the obvious. I remember once when my younger brother was furiously looking for his glasses and he got angry because we kept laughing at him. The reason was that he had them on!

If you listen very carefully, you can feel the energy behind someone's questions. You can sense in their tone of voice and through their body language that this is a personal question. In other words, they are talking about themselves. When that happens, ask them, "What is the statement behind your question?"

5. What did you notice was the group's reaction as you were talking? Would you like to know?

This helps the speaker to notice the reactions to what he/she is saying. We call this "intent and impact." Often we defend our good intentions, but fail to honor the impact of our words or actions on others. In asking, "Would you like to know?", it helps the participant learn about their impact on others, and allows them to practice telling the truth and how it affected them.

Reflective Inquiries (Past/Present) Helping the participant reflect on past experiences and how they influence who they are today.

1. What's familiar about this?

I often ask this question because so many participants' everyday experiences are reminiscent of similar past experiences. When asking this question, ask for a show of hands. That way, you will know who to go to next and the group can see how many are similarly affected. The show of hands also lets the audience see who is not affected, which brings up the question, "Why not?"

2. What were you like when you first came here and what are you like now?

This allows participants to reflect on how they have changed because of some oppressive attitude or behavior, and for audiences to bear witness to the effects of being victimized.

3. What do you leave at the door?

I started using this question after it was mentioned in Last Chance for Eden by Debbie Eriacho. It is a profound question, so be ready for the intense emotions that this question elicits. Very much like the question above, this is another way to allow some folks to share what they have to go through to survive and what others don't have to face because of either their ethnicity or gender.

4. What does your company/agency lose when you can't be yourself?

This is especially helpful because it reveals how some folks are just a "shell" of who they could be because of what has happened to them. Be prepared, because this section is often a shocker to those who think that everything is going great. The idea is to encourage folks to ask questions such as these, if they really want to know what is going on in their relationships and workplaces.

5. What angered you about what happened?

Often anger is one of the emotions that is most feared in workplaces. However, avoiding or trivializing its importance often creates an escalation of the problem. Someone once said that to tame a wild bull is to give it a wider field. But anger is more than just having the freedom to express it – it is also about being believed and understood. That is why when someone expresses their anger, it is good to have folks repeat what they've heard and to share whether they understand what the anger is all about.

6. What hurt you about what happened?

Many times, underneath one's anger is a hurt that has been invalidated. Validate the hurt and you're halfway there. Also, along with validation comes the willingness to see your part in the issue and to take responsibility for your action or inaction.

7. I was just imagining what it must have been like for you…

This section is what I call setting up the "ambiance" of the situation. I do this to bring the participant back to the scene of the crime in order to find some kind of healing or understanding. This section requires good storytelling skills and emotional affect. For example, "As I was listening to you, I could see your daughter is bright eyed and excited to go to college….and then, as a father myself, I was just imagining how hard it must have been for you to hear that they experienced the same kind of racism that you did…"

8. How did it affect you when it happened? How did it feel? How does it affect you now? In your workplace? In your relationships? How do you compensate for it so that no one knows?

These questions are all related – they lead from the past to the present. The last one is especially important because it reveals how a person compensates for their fears and experiences. It is useful because what this person needs is support, compassion and understanding.

Action Inquiries: Actions that the participant would like to see happen that would improve relationships and/or conditions.

1. If you could say something to_____, what would you say?

This question allows the participant to be direct with the person who is affecting his/her life, be it through their anger, hurt, fear, etc. It is a way of going back to the scene of the crime and getting a second chance. In a sense, it is a way of reclaiming and completing an unfinished part of themselves so they can go on with their lives. It is not so much the outcome that is of importance, but the process and the empowerment that it engenders.

2. If you could tell _____ what you need to be able to stay here, what would you say?

This affords the participant an opportunity to share what they need, which they may or may not have been aware of at the time or were too afraid to say. It is a chance to declare that they are important and deserving of being heard and acknowledged.

Facilitators often jump to this question of "need" because they don't want to deal with the emotions of anguish and hurt that could emerge. My experience is that males often reach for this question first because they are enculturated to come up with a solution quickly and to avoid processing emotions. This is also a very Western approach, as opposed to many other cultures. This is a useful question after some important emotional processing has taken place. Remember that we as facilitators often only go as far as our own experiences. If we are afraid of conflict, we will also restrict how far we will allow a group to express themselves.

3. What makes it unsafe for you here? Tell the group.

This is not an easy question. It will take a lot of bravery because it means revealing what is not safe. Once what is not safe is revealed and believed, then it will pave the way to express what will make it safer. This is also an opportunity for the audience to share whether they are willing to make this a safer work environment or not. In reality, this is really a community question and statement about whether or not it truly desires to create a multicultural environment where everyone is valued and honored.

Often the lack of safety exists because no one talks about the real issues or problems. Silence doesn't breed more safety, but rather promotes the myth that the truth is something to be feared or avoided.

Given the fragile nature of this question, in terms of reprisals, use extreme tenderness and compassion in your tone of voice and body language. This is risky business – especially for the participant. What she/he is doing requires great courage and honesty. Be respectful and supportive.

At the end of his/her statement, acknowledge the speaker. I often tell the agency/audience that he/she is the heart and conscience of their agency. They are lucky to have this person, because he/she willing to tell the truth to make this workplace a safer and more productive environment for everyone.

4. What would make you feel safer here? Tell the group.

This is a good follow-up question to the previous one. However, it requires having faith and hope. The question of safety is important to this process because it implies the importance of change along with an acknowledgement that something has not worked and has harmed some of the participants in this agency. Too often we move towards a solution before the problem has been acknowledged and responsibility taken.

If some participant(s) share that nothing would make them feel safer, two approaches might be helpful. Acknowledge to the audience that often this is the product of years and years of unkept promises and unfulfilled diversity goals. Then ask what they would do if they were the President of the agency. Both are revealing.

Some individuals in the agency may be contemplating leaving because they have given up hope of change ever happening. This process reinforces the need to act and to initiate change before it is too late. I often ask for a show of hands of those who want this person to stay. This helps create a sense of community and hope.

Mindful Facilitation Inquiry Guide
Group's Reactions

Observational Inquiries

1. What did you notice as _____was talking?

This is an important question because it trains the group to practice noticing body language, feelings, and content and then to correspond it to the context of what someone has shared. For example, "I noticed when you talked about your mother, you looked down." This question to the group is especially useful when someone says they feel invisible or unimportant.

2. What did he/she say? What did he/she not say?

It is unusual for folks to listen for what someone has not said. This helps audiences train to listen for the whole of what someone says, rather than just the parts. For example, "I noticed you talked about your father a great deal, but not about your mother."

3. I notice you had a *reaction* when _____ was talking.

This is a way of gauging the impact of what someone has said or done. It trains the audience to pay attention to intent and impact. For example, "I noticed when Tom was saying he felt very hurt, you kept nodding with tears in your eyes."

4. What did you hear in _____'s voice?

This trains the audience to listen for tonality and emotion in someone's voice, instead of just content and intent. This question is especially important to ask the audience when someone feels unheard and unacknowledged.

5. What *just happened* here?

This question allows the audience to notice and to share what they see as the intent and impact of someone's communication process. In a larger sense, it helps the disputants see more clearly how they are being perceived, which may not happen otherwise because they are emotionally involved.

Reflective Inquiries (Past/Present)

1. What was your *reaction* when _____was talking?

This intervention helps the speaker become aware of the impact of their communications and to allow for similar reactions to be expressed.

2. What is *familiar* about all this?

This question is meant to elicit similar feelings and experiences so they can be expressed and shared, thereby dispelling the speaker's feelings of isolation and aloneness.

3. What was *hard* about what happened and what was *good* about it? Why?

This question is often asked so that the audience can help define what happened more clearly and how the effects can be possibly beneficial.

4. What *moved* you about what just happened? Why?

This allows the emotional effect of an experience to be expressed and shared so that a sense of community can be developed and nurtured.

5. What *isn't* being said here? What's familiar about that?

This allows the audience to practice noticing what isn't being said and the effect it has on what they are witnessing. It also sets the stage for the audience to share how their own life stories are being triggered by what is happening in the room.

6. How many of you know *exactly* what he/she is talking about? Why or why not?

Like the question above, it allows those who have had similar experiences to share their life stories and what it has taken for them to get to this room. It also allows the group to notice who doesn't have to go through these experiences and to find out what those reasons are. I often call these disparities "the two Americas."

Action Inquiries:

1. How many of you want _____ to stay here? Please raise your hands. How many of you are willing to work towards some of the changes that he/she was talking about?

This question assists the agency in making a commitment towards change. It also helps make the speaker feel heard and validated.

2. What are you willing to do today to unlearn racism here at this workplace?

This supports the individual in reflecting on their actions and evaluating the impact they may have on the rest of their co-workers. It also encourages the individual to act today, rather than waiting for change to arrive or to rely on someone else to save them. In the words of Ghandi, "Be the change that you want to see in the world."

3. What did you learn about yourself today that will be helpful in unlearning racism? What did you learn about others today?

This question helps foster a sense of community and the desire to act together for the mutual benefit of everyone. It also promotes self-reflection and personal responsibility.

Mindful Facilitation Techniques

Positioning

When talking with a participant it is important to be mindful of where to stand in relation to them, because it can impact the degree of trust and sense of safety they feel towards you. Try to stand at a forty-five degree angle so that the speaker can sense your involvement and support while at the same time keeping you within eyesight of the group and your co-facilitator. Choosing which side is dependent on where your co-facilitator is positioned. Try to stand in a position across from each other so that your line of vision isn't impaired by the group or the speaker.

The question often comes up about how close to stand. Some facilitators ask the participant. I usually do this intuitively. Often a person's receptivity to me is expressed long before I even walk up to them. There is no set rule. Trust yourself and be aware of the other person. Pay attention to your own body language. If you are unsure of yourself or pretending to be relaxed, that pretense will be communicated. Be real. Sincerity *creates* trust. For example, I have often shared with groups that I felt nervous because I was the only Asian person in the whole room – an experience I have had most of my life. The result is that I often have felt self-conscious and withdrawn.

Authentically Relating

When I am standing next to someone who wants to talk, I always greet them in some way. I'm never quite sure what I'm going to say, but most of the time I say, "Hello." At other times I might say, "How are you doing? And your name is...." I do this because I am relating to a person, not just a "participant." To me, they are not an object, and what they are going to share with me will take a lot of courage and the willingness to be vulnerable in front of their peers. So be respectful and be honored. They are about to offer you a rare gift – their most heartfelt truth: their life story.

One more important note: When a participant is angry with me, I always walk up and address them by their first name. I do this for several reasons. Most of the time it is to bring us closer to each other, not only in proximity, but in a less adversarial way. Too often we are enculturated to behave in a "mob" mentality when we have the protection of being anonymous in a large group. Standing next to the other person puts a face onto our stereotypes and allows for a personal exchange – talking *with* each other, rather than *at* each other.

For effective communication to take place, it must be with the recognition that each of us holds a *part* of the truth. Hearing another's truth is an essential part of the wholeness of a healthy relationship.

Someone once said, "Fear is a natural reaction to moving closer to the truth." However, it is important to acknowledge the fear in opening ourselves up to another person, let alone to all of our peers. It is also important for a facilitator to acknowledge his/her own fears, too. Often a participant is only a mirror of ourselves. My sense is that we are *all* participants and teachers at any given moment.

Listening and Responding Mindfully

Listening is a lifetime opportunity. Listening *and* responding mindfully requires being present and open. When responding mindfully, I would like to suggest these three basic techniques:

Reflective Listening: Repeating verbatim back to the speaker as many significant statements that you heard and can remember. You are essentially recalling what was said – the facts of what happened. For example. "What I heard you say was..."

Empathetic Listening: Empathetically sharing with the speaker what you have heard. This is also an opportunity for the listener to communicate understanding and compassion for what the speaker has experienced or is going through. For example, "I could really sense how painful this must have been for you."

Non-Verbal Listening: Observing the messages that are not spoken in words, but physically communicated. For example, "I noticed that you started to slump each time you talked about your father." Non-verbal listening also means noting any statements or thoughts that weren't talked about or were indirectly referenced. This includes any questions that might also have a statement behind them.

Closure & Disclosure

I think that quite often companies won't do relationship work in seminars because they're afraid of not being able to achieve closure. I have a different perspective. I think the real fear is not so much about how to achieve closure, as it is the fear of what to do if there is *too much disclosure*. My experience tells me that very few institutions know how to deal with intense emotions, let alone conflicts that might occur about race, gender, or sexual orientation.

As a therapist and diversity trainer I think it is important to explore the different aspects of closure. My observation of most conflicts is that they are based on three major needs: to be accepted, to be acknowledged, or to be understood. Through the act of listening and responding, the participant feels believed and understood.

Most therapists will tell you that the real healing process *begins* with one's willingness to disclose – to go back to what I call "the scene of the crime." It is there that the real courage lies, the real trust in taking the first step backward. Often the unfinished business concerning discrimination is about feeling alone and isolated with one's pain, of being betrayed or discriminated against without just cause or reason, or feeling blamed.

In our trainings and seminars, people of color and women feel a tremendous permission and need to talk about what has happened to them because of the model of disclosure offered in our films. The participants' memories of their past experiences are stimulated and they are returned to the unfinished emotions of their past experiences. Often their unfinished business is about *not* being able to grieve or to get angry at the perpetrator, or to be validated by the institution in a way that allows them to move on emotionally and professionally with their lives.

The healing that is needed often comes in two phases: The first is what I call the "release stage" – being able to articulate in words and/or emotionally what happened. The second is the "reclaiming stage" – a process where the victim is able to take back what was taken from them, for example, their dignity and respect. In the reclaiming stage, their community of peers has the opportunity to offer validation and understanding, as well as the choice to take whatever action the victim feels is needed for he/she to heal. That "action" can take many forms. Some participants have shared that just being believed was sufficient, while others have asked for and gotten assurances that their peers would step forward and say or do something if this were ever to happen again.

One woman shared in one of our seminars that this was the first time she had ever shared what had happened to her, and that it was such a relief to finally tell her story and not have it be seen as inappropriate or invalidated. As Thomas Paine once wrote, "All the truth really ever wants is to be heard."

Intent and Impact

One of the major goals of mindful facilitation is noticing the communication process. All communication has an *intent* and an *impact.* The art of mindful facilitation is to learn the *intent* behind a communication and to notice what *impact* the communication has on those listening. *Intent* is really the "why" behind one's communication. It is the history of one's experience being expressed. The *impact* is the result of one's intentions. It is "what happens" to the listener(s) when someone has said or done something.

When one can learn "why" someone acts the way they do (because of some past experience), they can better understand the context of their responses and also have more compassion for what it has taken for them to get to where they are now.

Similarly, learning how *what* we say or the *way* we say something impacts the listener(s) can give us valuable information on how effective or ineffective we are in our communications with others.

Most people are somewhat aware when someone or something has *impacted* a room. However, work environments usually have a culture that either encourages or discourages one from expressing one's personal observations or personal experiences. My experience has been that very few work environments offer the safety or the comfortableness to allow people to communicate on a personal or emotional level. Often the focus is on the completion of a task or the viewing of issues from a purely solution-oriented perspective, and not on the root causes.

Learning how to *integrate* the usefulness and importance of working from both an emotional and an objective perspective is where the real transformation of an organization often needs to take place. Learning about the emotional state of one's staff can often lead to understanding the deeper reasons for high turnover rates, or individuals who are continuously out on sick leave, as well as company lawsuits concerning racism or sexual harassment. One's emotional and physical well being are seldom separate.

The Art of Mindfully Interrupting

When someone is talking and you need to interrupt, there are many ways to intervene without breaking the flow of the conversation. Here are some interventions that might be helpful:

"I'd like to help you here..."

"You've said a lot. What I'd like to do is to take in what you've just shared. What you said was..."

"Did anyone notice what just happened here?"

"Before you go any further... how are you feeling about what you've just shared?"

"I want to ask you a question before you go on any further. Have you noticed any one's reaction to what you've said? Why or why not?"

"Before you go onto another story, can anyone in the audience tell me one thing that he/she said that deeply moved you?"

"Take one more minute."

Creating Transitions

Transitioning from one speaker to another is an art form. It requires a facilitator to have a sensitive ear and eye, as well as an ability to listen to the subtle connections within a communication.

Here are some helpful transition techniques:

1. Be aware of the *similarities* between the various speakers.

2. Use the audience to notice the *differences* between the various speakers.

3. *Summarize* what is being said and what is *not* being said.

4. Share your observations about *similar* or *different* body language.

5. Always find a way to transition back to the *primary speaker* using the above suggestions.

6. If the primary speaker talks about feeling "invisible," find another participant that "sees" him/her.

7. If the primary speaker talks about feeling "unheard," use the audience or another participant to repeat back what they heard.

8. If the primary speaker is discouraged, have another participant or certain members of the audience that might be of the same ethnicity or gender come up and offer their support.

9. Always remember to *summarize* after each major experience to help educate the group on the subtleties of the communication process. This will help the group in practicing similar interventions in the future.

The Art of Listening

"To die, but not to perish, is to be eternally present."

~Buddhist Proverb

1. Listen to what is being said and what is not.

2. Observe the language of the body.

3. Notice *how* something is being expressed and what *words* are used.

4. What you *feel* is as important as what you hear and see.

5. Be willing to adapt and to adjust to the moment.

6. Notice how your body and words express your projections.

7. Notice when you are asleep and why.

8. Keep breathing. Allow space for humor, warmth, and grief.

9. Compassion is one of the highest forms of being present.

10. Acknowledge and utilize the wisdom that is in each person.

11. Accept and validate the truthfulness of each person's perception.

12. Notice where someone begins and ends.

13. Notice what is in the middle of the room.

14. Model the acceptance and openness to conflict, anger, and pain.

15. Acknowledge the courage and intimacy of being vulnerable.

16. Be kind to yourself and others.

Conflict Facilitation Model

Instructions:

        Identify who has an issue with someone else.
        Check to see if they want to resolve the issue or not.
        Check to see where the disputants want to sit.

Safety Guidelines:

        No interrupting.
        No threats or violence.
        Confidentiality.

Facilitator explains that one person will speak first and the other will listen and repeat back what they have heard. Each will have a chance to speak.

Facilitator (to speaker): *What happened? What angered you about what happened?*

Facilitator (to listener): *What did you hear_____say?*

Listener (After repeating what speaker said): *Did I leave anything out?*

Facilitator (to speaker): *What hurt you about what happened?*

Facilitator (to listener): *What did you hear_____say?*

Listener (after repeating what speaker said): *Did I leave anything out?*

Facilitator (to speaker): *What do you need from_____?*

Facilitator (to listener): *Are you willing to do that? Why or why not?*

Facilitator (to speaker): *Do you believe her/him ? Why or why not?*

Facilitator thanks each disputant and summarizes each disputant's contribution and what will be needed in the future for them to continue in their relationship with each other.

Facilitating A Conflict
By Lee Mun Wah

1. Breathe. Notice how you are *feeling.*

2. When you are not sure what to say or do – be *still.*

3. Allow for *silence* after the speaker has shared.

4. *Mirror back* the concerns and feelings of the speaker.

5. *Non-verbally* acknowledge the feelings of the speaker.

6. Connect with the speaker using your eyes and body and voice.

7. Use your ethnicity, gender, etc. to make a connection with the speaker. Notice when all of these are also a threat or an obstacle.

8. Stay with the anger until it has been *fully* expressed. Then gently move towards the hurt.

9. Stay *connected* to your co-facilitator. Share the experience.

10. When one facilitator is listening, the other facilitator is observing the reactions of the group.

11. Ask about the *life context* of one's statements. Get to any past experiences. Discover how this affects the person today.

12. Watch for signs and clues that the group is leaving you. Notice and acknowledge their points of entry and departure.

13. Trust the wisdom of the group.

14. Conflict is an opportunity for intimacy. View anger as an intimate opportunity and a catalyst for change and illumination.

15. Let the participants tell you where to go next. It is their workshop.

16. Observe the Listener as well as the Speaker. Be aware of intent and impact.

 Workshop Issues

"It is the place of feeling that binds us or frees us."

~Jack Kornfield

Workshop Issues ~ Blame

The definition of blame is assigning responsibility for a fault or wrong. My experience with those who are heavily into blaming is that they are often feeling powerless and/or overwhelmed by some perceived wrong. As a consequence, something in their lives remains unfinished and continues to wound and stimulate them emotionally, physically, socially, and/or politically.

Inquire whether they are blaming an individual, a group or an institution. This is worth looking at because the perpetrator or institution may be unavailable for dialogue, which therefore brings about feelings of depression and hopelessness.

One aspect that I have noticed with those who are into blaming, is their inability to be direct with their own feelings. Hence, they are often left with unfinished feelings, fostering resentment and anguish.

Something also worth exploring is what kinds of "rewards" do they get from being "victimized"? On the other side, what is lost from their lives when they are unable to feel relaxed and safe?

Suggested Interventions:

1. Through the use of role play, have the participant confront their perpetrator(s) by choosing audience members who most closely represent their perpetrator(s).

2. Have the participant share what they need or don't need to heal.

3. Ask the participant what effect this experience(s) has had on their lives. What have they "lost"?

4. Ask the participant what part of their perpetrator(s) is also a part of themselves?

5. Does the participant want a solution?

6. Explore what kinds of feelings they are withholding.

7. What is their individual, group or family history regarding this issue?

Workshop Issues ~ Grief

The definition of grief is deep sorrow. The state of grief is being overcome with deep sorrow.

Grief can be internal and/or external. It is also different for different cultures, as well as for women and men, the young and the old.

Grief can also carry sorrow and anger. The anger is rarely expressed. Often it is anguish at ourselves, but it is seldom safely expressed towards the perpetrator.

Suggested Interventions:

1. Try to help the participant identify what is the "loss" and the journey leading up to the loss.

2. Help the participant express the impact of their loss on their lives, family, and community.

3. How is the participant's grief expressed? How is it not expressed? Why?

4. How have they chosen to grieve? If they haven't, what is their fear of grieving?

5. What is unfinished for the participant and why?

6. What does the participant need? What does he/she not need?

7. What was the point of departure (when the participant may have left the scene of the trauma(s) emotionally and/or physically)?

8. Allow space for the participant to express her/his grief.

Workshop Issues ~ Denial

"Even if only a minority of one, the truth is simply the truth."

~Ghandi

The definition of denial is the failure to acknowledge an unacceptable truth or emotion or accept it into consciousness. Often it is used as a defense mechanism.

Denial often serves to protect something valuable that we sense is in danger.

If I deny the problem, I avoid the responsibility and the guilt it may bring with it.

Denial can be healthy for survival. It is, however, unhealthy when the problem no longer exists and we are still practicing denial.

Denial is also about fear of the unknown, of some perceived threat. A group of educators once told me that there were four major reasons why they did not want to hear the truth. They were:

1. I like keeping things familiar.
2. What if everything gets too emotional? I don't like getting angry or hurt.
3. I don't want to know the truth, because what if I'm responsible?
4. If I give people of color and women what they want, I will be out of a job.

Suggested Interventions:

Have the participant look at the individual or group he/she is in denial about. That way they can see the *impact* of their denial. It also helps so he/she can put a face to their fears and possibly stimulate a much-needed dialogue.

1. Ask, "What are the rewards or benefits from maintaining your denial?"

2. "Is there a fear of any personal responsibility?"

3. Try, "What keeps you from believing?"

4. Ask, "What are you protecting?"

5. Inquire, "If the veils were lifted, what do you think would happen?"

6. Notice if questions are used to mask a statement. What is the statement underneath your question?

7. Use the audiences' personal stories and reactions to get a reality check.

Workshop Issues ~ Hurt

The definition of hurt is to feel pain or distress. Being hurtful is to cause distress to someone's feelings.

Hurt is usually a painful experience that is often unfinished. It takes a lot of energy to suppress one's pain and to move on. However, that pain usually goes somewhere and can be triggered at any time by some familiar stimulus.

One of the manifestations of having been hurt is the fear of conflict. Another is the fear of being hurt and/or of hurting others.

Most participants deal with the present tense of a person's hurt rather than exploring the past context or the root of one's pain.

Suggested Interventions:

A participant who has been hurt often needs to retell their story, and in the process, be believed, understood and empathetically embraced.

The participant who has been hurt needs to go back to the "scene of the crime" – expressing what happened, how it affected them then and now.

When hurt is unacknowledged and invalidated, it becomes anger. Therefore, to move through our hurt is to allow it to be expressed and validated.

Someone once said that to tame a wild bull is to give it a wider field. Allow the hurt and the anguish to have a safe place to be expressed.

If the participant has a set script to describe their hurt, ask them what is familiar about this and what are the "rewards" for playing out this scenario once more?

Validation comes from having one's hurt listened to and believed.

Use audience responses (repeating what they heard and using the participant's name) to help the participant feel seen and heard.

If the participant is unable or unwilling to talk about their hurt, have the audience notice what happens when one feels unheard and unseen.

The trauma can cause people to withdraw inside of themselves or to blame themselves to keep from being hurt again.

To help someone return to the scene of the crime, try to reconstruct the period of time and the surroundings as close as possible. A good storyteller begins with good "props" by using keywords that the participant used. That way you will create an "emotional ambiance" that will translate into a trusting connection with the participant to travel with you.

Often it is easier for the participant to share what they don't need before they can identify what they truly need to heal.

Workshop Issues ~ Fear

The definition of fear is an unpleasant emotion caused by the belief that someone or something is dangerous, likely to cause pain, or a threat.

Someone once said that perception is reality. For fear to be healed, one needs to penetrate the "walls" that surround that fear.

Fear often is reinforced through similar experiences.

One of the manifestations of fear is generalizing the experience and associating it with other similar groups, situations and issues.

Fear may also be masked by shame – the feeling that we are the only one feeling this way and/or that we should be moving on.

Fear is often used as a rationale for action or inaction.

Some fears are important for survival, such as a fear of fire and heights.

Fear is founded – not unfounded – because it is based on our perceptions and experiences.

Suggested Interventions:

Have the participant share what happened. Define the fearful experience. Give it a face, a place and a voice.

What are the issues surrounding the fear(s)?

Find out what is needed and what is not needed.

What is the cost of their fears emotionally/physically?

What are the rewards and consequences of their fears being revealed?

Use of role play is helpful in confronting and re-framing past traumas.

Update the fear to the present tense. Are those fears still real or are they still rooted in the past? Are we still that "child" who was helpless and unprotected? How can the adult heal the wounded child (for example, through our children, co-workers, friends, relatives, etc.)?

Solicit "allies" to be supportive. Have the audience share similar fears and the

consequences of those experiences on their lives.

Have the audience share their feelings about hearing what happened. Validation and acknowledgement are important to keep the participant from feeling isolated and alone with his/her experience(s).

At times, some participants may not be able to talk about their fears. Some may be too tearful and/or traumatized. Have the audience sit with this silence and notice what happens when our fears are left unfinished.

Not talking about our fears does not make it safer. Sometimes it is the silence between our words that is unbearable. Sitting and being with that silence is also a part of the healing process.

Buddhists believe that there are really only two forces on earth – fear and love. Hatred and jealousy are often about fear. Wars are started because of fear. Then, perhaps, peace is about overcoming fear and walking through our fears together.

Workshop Issues ~ Hopelessness

The definition of hopelessness is feeling despair or inadequacy or incompetency about something.

When someone says they are feeling hopeless, there must have been a time when they were hopeful. What was the hope? What changed? How did it affect them?

Hopelessness is often characterized by betrayal, loss of trust, loss of faith, and being without hope.

For hope to be reclaimed, change is required.

If hopelessness means feeling incompetent and inadequate, then being hopeful means feeling adequate and competent.

Hopelessness is often identified by such phrases as "I don't care any more," "Who needs them?," "I've gotten used to not expecting things to change," "Why try?" The result is always going to be the same," "I'm a lifer here. I just do what's expected of me," "Nobody cares so why should I?," "I don't care what anybody thinks of me anymore. I'm just who I am."

My sense of hopelessness is that it comes from losing hope. So that part of the process of healing will require unveiling what that hope once was. From there, perhaps talking about the sense of betrayal or loss that was involved. And with that, the need to rail against what happened, to grieve, to suffer openly and to be supported for having the "right" to be hurt or angry.

My experience with those who have lost hope is that often they felt powerless and alone when the events happened. The subtext is that they wonder if anyone cared or noticed what had happened to them and why they didn't stand up or speak out to help them. We often witness something happening, but out of our fears or past experiences with conflict, we watch in silence while others suffer the consequences. For the victims, there is this residual sense of being alone, both in the experience and in the recounting.

What is essential to the healing process is offering validation. Not just in believing what happened, but to be emotionally moved by the wounding. To allow ourselves to be there with someone – to *see and feel their suffering* and the consequences of our silence, and to understand how we, too, have lost something. From there, perhaps we can build a relationship from sharing that moment together.

One cannot rush or push someone into becoming hopeful again until they are ready. It takes time and our commitment to "model" being a change agent to earn their trust again. Many times that "earning" comes from simply telling the truth – whether it is about our being afraid or about being the perpetrator. Telling the truth deepens a relationship. Not telling the truth often makes it unsafe and unhealthy.

Suggested Interventions:

Have these participants retell the events leading up to their sense of hopelessness.

Encourage them to share the impact that their hopelessness has on their lives and those close to them.

Ask them what they have "lost" because of their hopelessness.

Do they want to become hopeful again? What will it take? What needs to be changed?

What were they like when they first came here to this agency and how are they now?

What does the agency lose when certain members are feeling hopeless?

Ask the participants what angered and hurt them about what happened.

What are the risks of hoping again?

In the *Horse Whisperer*, the author writes: "The truth is always there. Saying it out loud, now that's the hard part."

Workshop Issues ~ Guilt

The definition of guilt is having committed a specified offense or crime; having failed an obligation. Guilt by association is guilt ascribed to someone not because of any evidence, but because of their association with an offender.

My observation of guilt in my workshops has been that there is often a feeling of regret accompanied by a feeling of helplessness. For example, a participant named Frank revealed that he felt guilty about not having stood up for his best friend, Tom, who is black, when a racist joke was told in a group. Tom was visibly upset and shaken, but Frank said nothing. Since then, Tom has not spoken about it to Frank, but their relationship has changed dramatically. Frank shared with the audience that he felt extremely guilty for what happened. As you can see, after the experience he felt powerless and had a lot of regret. The key here is to have Frank articulate his pain and what he wished he had done instead. From here, I shared with him that he could choose to meet with Tom and tell him how he felt and how he wanted to have acted differently. He was shocked by how simple the solution was and agreed to do it. You see, I merely heard his request in what he didn't say and what he wished he had said.

Suggested Interventions:

I believe that guilt is really "coagulated grief" – that it needs to be expressed and acted on for the individual to "move on" from the point that they were traumatized.

If the individual is unable to notice where they are stuck, ask the audience what they noticed and to share it with the participant. This way there is a sense that the community is there to support and help clarify what happened as witnesses and friends.

Guilt is often not a realtime experience. Rather, it is often rooted in and springs from past experiences that are only stimulated by some present day experience that looks similar. Take the time to excavate those past connections. They will illuminate the situation and allow for compassion and a deeper understanding of one's strong reactions to these past events.

Guilt is a natural part of all relationships. The key is acknowledging that guilt and taking responsibility for what has happened. Participants that feel guilty avoid having eye contact with the group. Encourage the participant to look up and at the group. Have the participant talk about what happened and what the effect is. Next, have the group share how they are now feeling towards the participant.

Workshop Issues ~ Anger

Anger is one of those emotions that most people fear. The dictionary defines anger as a strong feeling of displeasure or hostility. Buddhists believe that to have no enemies is to take no prisoners, thereby de-escalating the crisis. Anger can also be a catalyst for change and/or a means of destruction. Both are important ingredients in nature and in relationships.

The Chinese believe that a crisis is both danger and opportunity. I seldom hear of anger as an intimate part of relationships or as an important opportunity for growth. And yet, it is an inevitable part of all healthy relationships as is the process of reaching reconciliation. I view anger as an opportunity and as a window into many truths.

One of the prerequisites for dealing with anger is learning about how it was dealt with in your own life. That exploration and understanding will be invaluable to your helping others. You will only go as far as you have learned or not learned. Understanding our own histories with anger provides us with an opportunity to grow and to heal.

When anger is often expressed, it is because some hurt has not been acknowledged. When that hurt is unacknowledged, it becomes anger. Each person however, is longing to be acknowledged. Hence, getting to the hurt is the goal of working with someone who is angered. The rite of passage into the hurt is to first listen and to acknowledge the anger.

Someone once said that to tame a wild bull is to give it a wider field. We often expend too much energy and time trying to manage and prevent folks from expressing their anger. The real truth, though, is that the anger always goes someplace. Whether it is into the body, through being irritable, violent, abusive, uncooperative, or disinterested – it always recreates itself somewhere else; sometimes, to the point of causing physical harm to one's health.

Anger is a scary emotion to many participants. Acknowledge this aspect with your audiences because they often have stories that will justify their struggles and resistance. Hearing and empathizing with those stories collectively helps dispel the myth that they are alone and isolated.

Use the anger in the room as a catalyst to stimulate more discussion. It will lead to other emotions and stories. Transformation often requires a crisis to stimulate the need for change.

Suggested Interventions:

1. Have these participants fully express their anger verbally and emotionally, so that their words and their body match their anger. Then ask the audience what they observed.

2. If possible, have the participants identify who it is that they are angry with or about (without using names or identifiable descriptions).

3. Have them share what hurt them about the incident.

4. Ask the participants what they need and what they don't need. Invite the group to be a part of the solution by asking what they noticed.

Summary:

No one ever died in our workshops, but maybe what died was some of our fears and attitudes. Maybe what we learned today were ways to express our anger so that we can get on with our lives by having more authentic and honest relationships with each other.

Workshop Issues ~ Invisibility

Invisibility is often about not being seen, feeling invalidated, unacknowledged and unappreciated. Therefore, the importance here is helping the participant experience feeling seen, appreciated, acknowledged, and validated. Though it may seem very simplistic on paper, what is needed is multi-layered – such as having to hear and to believe their experiences, taking responsibility and being willing to act to see that it doesn't happen again.

Invisibility is also closely related to shame and guilt – a feeling that sometimes they are inadequate (shame) and may have been the cause for being invisible (guilt).

Invisibility is often an issue for ethnic groups, women and other minority groups. Part of the trivializing and denial occurs when they hear such things as, "Everyone feels invisible at some time", or that they are too sensitive or being too "ethnic".

Suggested Interventions:

1. Have the audience repeat back one thing they heard the participant say (this helps the individual and their concerns to become "visible").

2. Ask the participant how they felt about what happened to them and the effect it had on their lives when it happened.

3. When someone has experienced feeling invisible, there are often other partici pants who have had similar experiences. Solicit their responses. This keeps the participant from feeling alone in their experiences and reactions and allows others to understand the pervasive impact it has on one's life.

Summary:

As you witnessed today, there are many folks here who felt like (name of participant). If we don't acknowledge and value these participants' contributions, after awhile they will either leave for a better job or they will stay, but never feel they can express their full potential. In either case, the company loses and so do all of you. How many of you want him/her to stay? Then you need to let him/her know how much you value him/her and how much you want to listen to what he/she needs to stay here. The heart of a company has always been its employees, without whom no company could exist or survive. That can only happen when folks feel valued and rewarded for who they are and for what they can contribute.

Workshop Issues ~ Shame

The definition of shame is a painful emotion caused by a strong sense of embarrassment, guilt, disgrace, or unworthiness.

The difference between shame and guilt is that often the person feels like they are a shameful person. Whereas a person who feels guilty often feels it is because of a specific act or situation.

Often a person who feels shame looks down or averts their eyes when talking about their experiences. Have them look up, not only to "face" those around them, but to be seen and accepted and possibly forgiven.

Shame often "freezes" someone to the past and makes them feel powerless. The work is to have them relate about what happened and how it affects them today. This gives their shame a face and present tense reality.

Suggested Interventions:

1. When she/he is finished sharing, have the group notice the impact of what happened to her/him. Allow plenty of time for silence and reflection.

2. When she/he is finished talking, have the group repeat back what they've heard.

3. Ask the group if they have ever felt ashamed and didn't want anyone to know about it. If they are willing, have them share their personal stories.

4. Have the group share how they feel about what they've heard and how they now feel about this person. In the cycle of shame, a main cause is the feeling of unworthi ness. By having the group share how they feel about this person in a positive way, they offer acceptance and healing. By having the participant look up at the group, the cycle of personal shaming and isolation begins to be broken.

Summary:

We all have something of which we are ashamed or not proud. To go on with our lives, we need to take responsibility, forgive ourselves and others, and then try again.

 Training Vignettes

If we knew tonight we were going to go blind, we would take a longing, last real look at every blade of grass, every cloud formation, every speck of dust, every rainbow raindrop – everything.

~Pema Chodron

Training Vignettes – Instructional Guide

The Training Vignettes are divided into six parts:

Vignettes:

What follows are the actual vignettes as they occurred in workshops that Lee Mun Wah has facilitated. Pay close attention to the keywords in the vignettes for clues about the presenting issues. They may be entrances into possible interventions. There is a Buddhist saying, "Nothing is what it seems to be and everything is what it was meant to be."

Questions for the Facilitators:

These questions were created as suggestions to ask yourself or to use during trainings. They provide some insight into viewing the vignette from a mindful perspective. They can be answered orally or in written form, whichever is more convenient for a group discussion. Having participants write their answers encourages them to come up with an answer for themselves. For folks who have cultural issues about speaking out first or in a public forum, writing is more conducive to creating a sense of relaxation.

When opening these vignettes up for group discussion, allow for spontaneous discussions. Encourage everyone to speak their mind. There is no one approach here, but rather many possibilities and perspectives. The discussion can take place in a large group or in groups of four or less.

Lee Mun Wah's Thoughts:

This section is meant to aid the facilitator in viewing the vignettes from a deeper and more intimate cultural and facilitative perspective. I tried to be candid with my feelings as well as drawing on my many years of experience to illuminate the many issues a facilitator faces during challenging exchanges.

Perhaps this section is more like a mirror for myself and ultimately, for the participant. What made these insights so effective was that they were real and thoughtfully emerged out of my desire to be eternally present with each person in their time of crisis. Each experience was, for me, a journey taken together. The learning and the growing were often reciprocal and meaningful for both of us.

My personal experiences of both being a Chinese man and having gone through my mother's murder are significant, in that they helped me to understand more intimately the anguish and grief of being victimized. I learned to use my pain and fear as a way of deepening my compassion for the struggles of those I sought to help. In the process, what was unfinished in myself served as a bridge for others. I did not always know the answers when I started, but each time the wisdom of where to go next emerged because the participant or group always let me know the way. Buddhists believe that if one pays attention to the moment, the future emerges. If one pays too much attention to what is ahead, what is before us is missed.

Lee Mun Wah's Interventions:

When I was writing these interventions, I became acutely aware of how grateful I was that a lot of these interventions worked. But then again, if they hadn't, I would have just tried another and another…

Actually, whenever I am stuck or confused or just speechless, I have learned to just stop talking and thinking; much like erasing a chalkboard that has become too full. Sometimes when I close my eyes, I can see more clearly, just as when I remember to breathe, I can hear and feel what is around me and inside of me. The Japanese have a word for that state of mind – hokomok – seeing all around.

Many of these interventions I use quite often because they are very effective; others very seldom because they worked mainly for that moment and for that particular participant. Someone once told me that they used my intervention in *The Color of Fear* where I said, "What keeps you from believing?" and it didn't work. I looked at her with a smile and said, "What makes you think it would?" What I meant was that these interventions work most of the time because they are appropriate. They may or may not work all the time because all human beings are all different. There is no one way to work with someone, but there are many paths to connect with someone. Each takes time and patience and an openness of the heart and mind.

I share these interventions with you to widen your choices and to encourage you to seize the moment – not arbitrarily, but with clear attention to what lies before you: the voice and the life experiences of another human being. Within their stories and dramas lie the clues to their healing and the reason they are here with you at this moment. You have only to be present and to be a sensitive witness to their journey. The answers and the questions they pose are right before you – you have only to listen and to be still to hear them. Your role is not to provide the answers, but rather to illuminate the path that they have chosen or are afraid to choose. You see, it is not the telling of the truth that most people fear, but the consequences that might occur.

Group/Dyad Process Questions:

This section is used to help the group to process what has just transpired. It allows the group to talk about what came up for them and how their own personal experiences relate to what they just witnessed. The goal of this processing is to model what it takes to develop a relationship with someone through learning how to listen compassionately and attentively to another's truth.

Summary:

This is a time to bring all the stories and issues into a learning moment. It is a time to thank those who shared and to advocate for the changes that were voiced. The summary is also a form of closure because it weaves a thread of commonality and deeper understanding of what is happening at their organization and what is needed for folks to be heard and valued. For me, the summary allows for the group to envision what it is to be a community and to acknowledge how much they need each other. This is not an easy section for most facilitators because it demands remembering what has happened and bringing it all together in a matter of minutes. One way to practice summarizing is by telling stories to children. Storybooks for children have a wonderful way of bringing everything all together into a learning moment. I was an Asian folkteller and tarot reader for years. I had no idea that someday those experiences would serve me well. Ah, so much for foresight.

A Gun In The Mouth

A young Jamaican student, Thomas, shared how he was stopped by a deputy for no apparent reason other than driving in a white neighborhood. He was questioned with a gun in his mouth and eventually released without charges. He quickly sat down, shaken.

Immediately, the town sheriff jumped up and told the mostly white audience how dangerous it was to be a law enforcement officer— "We're always on duty and we're always on guard" —and how proud he was of his department in protecting the citizens of this county. The audience gave him a standing ovation. The sheriff quickly sat down after smiling to the audience and waving to everyone. Thomas looked down and away from the group.

Questions for the Facilitator:

1. What came up for you during this incident?
2. What's difficult about this situation?
3. Who would you choose to work with first? Why?
4. What are some of the keywords that are still ringing in your ears?
5. How did you feel about the sheriff?
6. How do you want this to all end up? Why?
7. What do you think Thomas needs? Why?
8. What do you think the sheriff needs? Why?
9. What are you afraid might not happen? Why?

Lee Mun Wah's Thoughts:

I would have liked to work with Thomas first, but the sheriff's behavior prompted an immediate response. It was not easy listening to the sheriff because he sounded all too familiar to me as a person of color – those who trivialized my experience by only talking about themselves. What was important here was to notice how I was feeling and why, because it would show up in what I didn't say and create a dissonance between my words and my actions. The work of a facilitator is to stay focused and neutral while being a container for as much information as possible. When I become too biased, the focus shifts away from the client's needs and onto mine.

Sometimes, a situation like this feels like being in the eye of a storm, but often that is where it is the most calm with the best view. As the sheriff was talking, I kept checking in with myself, "What do you see and what do you hear? What did you not hear and not see? Trust your instincts and don't be afraid to use your own experiences as a guide. Be still, listen, feel, and stay awake to the past and the present." The clues are everywhere.

Two things struck me immediately as the sheriff was talking. He was obviously feeling defensive about the department and his role as the sheriff. In doing so, he said something quite significant, "…that the police were here to protect and serve the citizens in this town." That statement alone, gave me a glimpse into a possible opening between the sheriff and Thomas. If that were true, then what of Thomas' "protection"? You see, my sense is that the sheriff did not see Thomas as a citizen, as a part of the community. As a person of color he was an outsider inside a white community. The challenge would be to use the sheriff's energy without escalating his denial and defensiveness and at the same time, bring about some validation to Thomas' traumatic experience. Not an easy balance.

Lee Mun Wah's Intervention:

One of the keywords in this story was that Thomas had a gun in his mouth. Physically and symbolically—he could not speak, and if he did, his life would be in danger. The goal, therefore is to help Thomas reclaim his voice so that he can express his anger and hurt at the injustice that happened to him. The connection between the sheriff and Thomas was the deputy. So I said to the sheriff, "You're not finished yet, you left something out. Come on back up here." He was curious, so much so that he came up to the front, though he was a bit cautious. I then asked Thomas to come up next to the sheriff. I did this because it was important to have the two face each other to diffuse the tension and to help create a more intimate dialogue between the two of them.

So often in Western culture, I have noticed that most people talk to each other from a distance, giving themselves permission to be more arrogant and insulting. I believe that this only adds to the detachment and the anger of both parties. My experience has been that when you bring two folks in conflict closer together in physical proximity, the energy changes. What they see, hopefully, is another human being, perhaps very much like themselves—afraid and hurt. There is now a face to their hurt and anguish, not just a group or an issue to hurl insults at, unabated.

Sometimes folks can be re-traumatized further if they are brought together. So it is important to be cautious and aware and to follow the emotional cues of each person. The question I had for the sheriff was, "You left a few things out. After hearing Thomas' story, don't you want to know who the deputy was?" I chose this question because that is what I would have thought of if I were the sheriff or Thomas. Yet, in my experience of this culture, we seldom ask questions or take personal responsibility. This society often deflects the problem and responsibility as someone else's fault – never its own. The sheriff was only a consequence of that modeling or that lack of modeling.

The sheriff was shocked at my question. He hadn't even thought of asking this question, and neither, I suspect, did most of the audience. He hesitated and then said, "Of course." However, I told him because of confidentiality and for legal reasons, he needed to ask Thomas after the workshop.

My second question to the sheriff was if he wanted to know how the gun incident affected Thomas. He thought about it, and then nodded reluctantly. "Ask him," I said. I did this so that the sheriff could model for the community what is needed when one truly listens to someone who has been traumatized or oppressed. I also did this for Thomas, because this was the part of the incident that he had internalized – that part of himself that was still stuck in that dark, lonely night. You see, I was taking Thomas back to the scene of the crime. By having him tell the sheriff and the community his story, it would help break the isolation and the horror of feeling so alone with his experience. It would give a face to what happened – only this time there would be witnesses, and he would have his chance to speak and to be seen. It would help "break the silence" and the doubts that he carried about what happened.

To help ease Thomas into sharing, I said to him, "I know this isn't easy for you, but you need to go back there, to that night with the deputy to take back what was taken from you." Thomas trembled for a moment and then told the audience how frightening it was and how he thought he was going to die on that night. There wasn't a dry eye in the room. He also shared how nervous he still gets whenever he sees the police now and that he has had nightmares since that night. I asked the sheriff to repeat what he heard and how he felt. Afterwards, he said, "It must have been really frightening." At that point, Thomas had tears in his eyes and so did the sheriff. I shared with the audience, "This is what racism does – it changes your life. As you can hear in Thomas' story, that experience is with him today as if it were yesterday, and until he is believed and something is done about it, he will never be finished with that night and neither will this community." Thomas nodded, looking down at the floor.

I then asked the two of them if they would be willing to get to know each other. They both agreed. I then asked Thomas if he would be willing to have the sheriff over for dinner. He laughed because he didn't think the sheriff would come. I asked the sheriff and he agreed. Thomas was surprised. I then asked the sheriff to imagine he was driving to Thomas' home and all the neighbors were looking out their windows wondering why he was there. I asked the sheriff if he was nervous yet and he said, "You bet I am." The audience laughed. I then told Thomas to imagine that the sheriff was ringing the doorbell

and that he was slowly walking towards the door. I asked him if he was nervous and he said, "Yeah, I am. Wouldn't you be? No sheriff has ever come into our house. In fact, no white person has ever come to our house."

From there, they both looked at each other laughing, because it was true for the sheriff, too – no person of color had ever come into his home. I shared with the audience that maybe being courageous is also being scared. I also shared with the sheriff that if he never went to Thomas' home, then he and Thomas would never be able to heal over what had happened with the deputy, and that if the sheriff didn't see that justice was done with the deputy, Thomas would tell his community. The consequence is that when the police department needed his community to support them, then they would probably not be there for them. The sheriff nodded and so did Thomas. They shook hands and hugged and the audience applauded them both, many with tears in their eyes.

(I chose to have the two of them meet for dinner because food often is a way for different cultures to connect. Coming into Thomas' home was a way for the sheriff to risk coming out his comfort zone and into Thomas' community – a place where Thomas was more in control and could define the environment. The other significance of their meeting was to find a way for them to begin a dialogue that rarely happens between law enforcement and members of the community. Often the relationship is crisis oriented and adversarial, at best.)

It is important to note that I followed this suggestion up with a much broader request – that the sheriff follow through with his investigation of the deputy – to bring justice to what happened. The ramifications of his action or inaction would ripple out into the community in terms of future support or indifference.

Group/Dyad Questions:

1. What came up for you during this discussion?

2. What's familiar about what transpired?

3. Who did you identify with—the sheriff and/or Thomas? Why?

4. Where was the turning point in this discussion between Thomas and the sheriff?

5. At what point were you scared during this exchange?

6. If you could say something to the sheriff, what would that be?

7. If you could say something to Thomas, what would that be?

8. What do you think it will take for this community to come together?

9. What do you think Thomas needed from his experience with the deputy?

10. Why do you think Thomas didn't report the deputy?

11. Do you think the sheriff will follow through with his investigation of the deputy? Why or why not?

12. What do you need from this community for you to feel there is justice here?

13. What is it like for you as a person of color/white person living here in this community?

Summary Points:

1. Acknowledge the sheriff and Thomas for their courage and risk taking and for staying in the room.

2. Acknowledge the group for being present and supporting the two participants, instead of taking sides, which would have added to the escalation of a situation.

3. Point out that merely hearing a victim's story is not enough. It requires empathy, compassion, understanding, and the willingness to act so that this situation and experience doesn't happen again.

4. A "community" means that everyone is important and needs to be a valued participant.

5. Share with the audience that the sheriff and Thomas need their support in following through with their commitments to each other...that it is so easy to just get back into daily life and to forget the importance of what happened today.

6. Encourage the audience to stay connected to the persons they paired up with today be it for a meal, a phone call, or to come over to each other's homes.

7. What transpired today wasn't easy. There was no model for them to follow except their willingness to try to hear each other. All healthy relationships have to endure someone getting hurt or angry or being misunderstood. The real work is staying in the room with each other instead of running away.

8. It is important to remember that when one of us falls, we all fall. When one of us rises, we all rise together as human beings and as a community.

Hiroshima

A EuroAmerican man, Harold, shared how he felt badly all these many years because he was part of the team that worked on the bomb that fell on Hiroshima. He said he felt a great deal of shame for what he did to so many innocent women and children. He still had a hard time sleeping or looking Asian folks in the face.

Questions for the Facilitator:

1. What came up for you in reading this vignette? Why?
2. What is Harold feeling? Why?
3. What are some of the keywords to focus in on?
4. Where would you begin? Why?
5. What does Harold need? Why?
6. What did he leave out?
7. What is familiar about Harold's story for you? Why?
8. Are you sympathetic or turned off by Harold? Why?
9. How would you include the participants in this situation? Why?

Lee Mun Wah's Thoughts:

As I was listening to Harold, I could see the guilt in his retelling, but also his need for something that his white colleagues could not give him – forgiveness. That could only come from someone who was Japanese. I saw a group of Asian folks, but I wasn't sure if they were Japanese. The only clue I had was this particular Asian couple who were crying. It was then that I realized that they could possibly be Japanese. They were an older couple, so the chances were good that they had either been in the camps or had relatives in Japan. I sensed there was some connection. The tricky part would be how to honor their privacy and to not use them as objects for a history lesson or as a confessional without their permission.

Something that I noticed was that when Harold mentioned innocent women and children he did not mention the men. Once again, it reminded me of how people of color are seldom seen as individuals, but rather as groups, and never as Americans. So once again, "All the American men attacked Pearl Harbor" and not just those involved. "All Japanese Americans were spies and loyal to Japan," therefore, they all needed to be interned.

The issue of WW II was not just about being at war, but also about the dehumanization process of caging Japanese Americans. Furthermore, it was about demonizing the Japanese enough to justify dropping a bomb to shorten a war while making no mention that it would kill innocent civilians – men, women, and children. So the issue here is more than just this particular war, but also who is an American and who is a foreigner? Who were the barbarians and who were the victims?

Harold's ability to look up and allow himself to be seen became a goal to offset his sense of "hiding" behind the bomb that was dropped. Someone said that guilt is simply coagulated grief. Guilt is a natural part of the life experience, but it can also be paralyzing. Along with guilt must come responsibility, forgiveness, and the willingness to try again.

Lee Mun Wah's Intervention:

I asked Harold how his experience affected him and what he needed in order to get on with his life. He said, "Forgiveness."

I then asked if there were any Japanese in the audience and three stood up. I asked Harold to share with them how he felt. He shared how ashamed he was about what he had done, and that he wanted to tell them how sorry he was for having participated in something that killed so many innocent folks.

Some of the Japanese folks told him they appreciated his apology and some said they didn't need it nor were they looking for it. They just wanted him to be aware that it happened and the harm that the internment caused to so many who felt they were loyal Americans. To them, the greatest tribute he could give them was to make sure it never happened again to anyone. The couple and Harold, with tears in their eyes, bowed to each other.

Group/Dyad Process Questions:

1. What moved you about this exchange? Why?

2. What do you think most victims want or need? Why?

3. What is unfinished in you? How has that affected who you are now?

4. What was the turning point for Harold?

5. What did you appreciate about Harold? Why?

6. How did you feel about the Japanese couple? What came up for you?

7. What came up for you about Hiroshima?

8. What are your feelings about the Japanese internment?

9. What's familiar about this experience?

10. What did you learn from this experience?

Summary:

1. Thank all the participants who shared: Thank Harold for his honesty and openness, as well as the Japanese folks in the audience for their openness and graciousness.

2. Note that the Japanese internment left many disillusioned, homeless and jobless, and that it financially ruined many generations of Japanese families.

3. Ask the Japanese family why they forgave Harold. What was it about his apology that moved them? Be aware that they may not look at him because of their cultural traditions and out of respect.

4. Note that though Harold wanted forgiveness, he first took personal responsibility for his part in the problem and then was willing to be part of the solution.

5. Recognize that the deeper question is who is an "American" and who is not?

6. Continue the work by talking and sharing. The hard work is to look at our part in promoting or supporting racism by not doing or saying anything when it occurs.

Martin Luther King Jr. was right: "What will be remembered is not the words of our enemies, but the silences of our friends."

The Color of My Fear

Prior to doing this workshop, my co-facilitator, Linda, an African American woman, and I were threatened by a letter sent to my home. We were told that if we did the workshop we would be shot. This was the one and only time I had ever been threatened. On the day of the workshop we were escorted into the room by security guards. Participants were searched at the door.

A EuroAmerican man wearing sunglasses would not let Linda begin the workshop until she answered whether or not she had a diversity training license. Linda tried to convince him that she had a Masters Degree in Counseling and five years of experience in diversity work, but he maintained his questioning, badgering her "Do you or don't you have a license in diversity?" She finally said, "Then you must know there is no license in diversity." He then became increasingly insulting, " You have nothing to show us or tell us about…that shows that you have some sort of credentials…You could be a waitress, be a worker…in Sloppy Joe's." . Linda became incensed, "If you want to do this, I'd welcome you to come up and do it." The man hesitated and then asked me whether or not I had a license. Without giving me a chance to answer, and referring to me as 'Man Wah', he said, "He's being inscrutable."

Questions for the Facilitator:

1. What came up for you in this vignette? Why?
2. What was hard for you about this vignette? Why?
3. What are some of the keywords to focus in on?
4. What do you think is angering Tom? Why?
5. At what point did Linda get "hooked"? Why?
6. What do you think Tom wants?
7. What is not being said?
8. What do you think is needed here?
9. How can you include the participants in this conversation?
10. Who would you work with first? Why?
11. What is frustrating about Tom?

Lee Mun Wah's Thoughts:

I believe that every facilitator or trainer, if they are truly honest with themselves, carries an image of someone they most fear will show up in their workshop. I was no exception. For a long time, I carried within me a fear that I would someday meet someone like my father. Someone who was powerful and charismatic and loud enough to make me feel worthless and inarticulate. Someone who wouldn't let me talk or continue on with the workshop and who knew my deepest doubts about myself.

It has been my experience that what we do not face or deal with confronts us again and again throughout our lives – in the form of employers, enemies, friends, or lovers. We seem to carry this false mythology that if we don't talk about our fears, they will go away. But, it has been my experience that our lives are made more unsafe when we don't face our fears – that we give them more power and energy than they deserve through our silence and our denial.

For the first time in my life, I feared for my family. In looking back, I was surprised that I gave very little thought about myself, until members of my staff became worried for my safety. I guess it was the Asian side of me stepping in once again – putting the welfare of others before my own.

When the day of the workshop finally came, there were security officers at the door checking for concealed weapons. Strange, I was more afraid of the weapons they carried inside of them. A gun at least lets you know where they stand – the heart is more prone to concealment, and therefore, much more dangerous.

The first thing I noticed when I came in was how narrow the room was and how hard it was to breathe. This place was like a prison. No window, with barely enough room to walk or hide. Escape, of course was out of the question, but very much on my mind. A voice kept nagging at the back of my mind, "Is this the day?"

When I looked around at the faces in the room, I could sense the tension was building. There was a scattering of folks of color, but like most of our seminars, this was the norm – 20% or less of people of color and always more than 80% white. And then I saw him. My worst fears were personified. Sitting right in front of me was a white man, wearing sunglasses and sitting loosely in his chair with a swagger that befitted his arrogance. He was in charge and everyone around him was aware of his presence and the power he wielded. It didn't take much to recognize that this could really be a long day or a short one for one of us.

I turned away and quickly walked outside to the hallway, trembling. I was truly afraid. Afraid that this could be the day that all of my experiences and knowledge would be for naught. That he would have his way with the audience and I would be left looking helpless and humiliated. I cried and prayed to my mom who was murdered in 1985, as well as my ancestors, to help me….to give me strength and the wisdom to make it through this day. As I was praying, I could hear myself – one part of me believing and the other part paralyzed with fear that maybe no one would be there when the time came.

As my co-facilitator, Linda, introduced herself and explained why we were here, she was abruptly interrupted by the man with the sunglasses. "Excuse me. I have a question." All eyes turned to him, the same way a siren wakes us up to the possibility that something dangerous is close at hand. As the room resonated with a deafening silence, I could feel the dryness in my throat – a warning that an absence of words was a very real possibility.

Linda asked what his question was. With a loud and authoritative voice, he asked her the kind of question that doesn't want to be answered, because the answer has already been decided. "Do you have a license to do diversity?" As Linda struggled to explain that there was no license for diversity and that her Masters in Counseling along with her years of experience were sufficient, I could tell that she knew that he already knew the answer and this was just an elaborate trap to get her to disclose it publicly. "So," he said, "We're expected to sit in here with someone who doesn't have a license to do diversity and who might traumatize some of us or even worse. We should have been warned that you weren't properly credentialed. How many of you were aware they didn't have a license?"

Linda and I have a joke about this kind of situation. It's called, "Glad I'm not you." She would often tell me this whenever I told her about a difficult audience I had just finished with. I thought about what she said and was relieved it wasn't me, and then realized that in just a few seconds he was coming after me. So much for the idea of gathering my thoughts by going second. I was on next even though I wanted to run, or at the very least, to go amnesiac for just a few minutes. Ah, the gods do laugh when they give us what we want.

Lee Mun Wah's Intervention:

When the man with the sunglasses finally did ask me for my license, too, I realized that there was no use repeating to him how good a person I was or that I had even more credentials than Linda. In paralyzing moments like these, everything feels like it's in slow motion; only as a facilitator, there's no time to dwell on the esoteric meaning of it all. Everyone is waiting for you to say something that will somehow make everything okay or at the very least, to go back to the way it was before. In diversity training, we call this "the elephant in the middle of the room." No way around it anymore – it's too late. The time to deal with it is now.

Most trainers will tell you that you gotta do something at this point. In this case, I needed a little more time. At first, I thought I just needed time to assess what to do, but then it occurred to me that what I was feeling was that there was something familiar about this exchange. And so to buy a little time, I blurted out, "I would be glad to answer your question, on one condition." After I said this, I realized that I had no idea of any condition, let alone one condition. BUT, it did buy me a few valuable seconds, because everyone just stared at me with absolute anticipation and curiosity.

So, as I slowly walked towards him, along the way, I realized that I was angry at him. But angry at what? I didn't even know him. And then it came to me. I was angry because this scene was all too familiar to me. I had seen it again and again happening to people of color and women and gays and lesbians and to those who were poor and without power – always having to prove that we're good enough, smart enough, experienced enough or professional enough to a white man. And so….I said to him, "Would you have asked me for my credentials or license if I were a white man?" The room was stunned by my question and maybe even more because it was the truth.

He leaned back and to my amazement, said, "Okay, you got me." His response caught me off guard. I was stunned at how fast and willing he was to admit what he had done. But, then I realized that on the surface, this sounded pretty good, didn't it? Another Kodak moment. But, to dwell here would be letting the rest of the room off the hook. I didn't want this to just be about the both of us. I had to find a way to bring it back out to the rest of the group so that it would be a learning opportunity for everyone. And so, I told him, "I wasn't out to get you, I just wanted you to get a sense of what it is like for folks of color to prove on a daily basis that they're just as good as anyone else. How many of you in this room know what I am talking about? Please stand." All the folks of color stood up, as well as all the women. Most of the white men were sitting. From here, the stories just poured out from the people of color. Unwittingly, Tom was the catalyst for something larger than the two of us – what it was really like here at this agency and in this country, on a daily basis, as a person of color.

When my worst fear finally happened, what transpired changed my life. It was perhaps, the day of my reckoning. And what I learned not only saved my life, but created a template – using what had hurt me in my life to create a deeper understanding when it happened again. But that was only afterwards. When I was going through it, I felt like I was in the eye of the storm and that my life was at stake.

Perhaps Buddhists are right, that a crisis can either be seen as danger or an opportunity. I would probably say that today was a "dangerous opportunity" that helped us all come to a deeper understanding of each other and the differences between us.

Group/Dyad Processing:

1. What came up for you when you were listening to this unfold?
2. What's familiar or unfamiliar to you in this story?
3. What hurt/angered you about this story?
4. What scared you about this story? Why?
5. What inspired you about this story? Why?
6. What are your fears of a particular group or person?

Summary:

1. Thank all those who shared.

2. The real work here is to realize that when conflict occurs it is important to truly listen to each other and to learn what it has taken for someone to get to this room. Along with this is our willingness to stay in the room when it hurts or when we are misunderstood. All healthy relationships require work.

3. It was not who was wrong or right here today, but rather what causes us to treat each other so differently. What have we learned that causes us to fear or to doubt an other's abilities and intelligence?

4. How willing are we to learn about each other's differences and not just what we have in common? In other words, it is time to get outside of our familiar world and to explore those places we have never been to and with people who look and act and think differently from ourselves.

5. These are the two Americas. Which one are you a part of? And what are you doing to end racism on a daily basis?

This wasn't just a Kodak moment – it was a taste of what life is really like, day in and day out, for people of color and so many others all over this country. Having to prove that they are good enough and smart enough.

James Baldwin was right. America is one tough town.

I Can't Believe You Said That!

I was doing a workshop on Unlearning Racism and Sexism and during the break a EuroAmerican man, Ken, shared with me that his daughter was applying for a job at a rival company and that he was very proud of her.

Before we began the second half of the workshop, I encouraged the group to tell the truth. Ken got up and shared that all women were good for was to have babies and to open their legs. A young African American, Eve, ran out the workshop screaming and crying, "I can't believe you said that!" Ken was shocked and yelled out at me and the group, "You tell us to tell the truth and now look what happened. I'm not saying anything else!" The rest of the group was stunned, not knowing who to help first, Eve or Ken.

Questions for the Facilitator:

1. What came up for you in reading this vignette? Why?
2. How did you feel when Eve ran out? Why?
3. What is hard about this story? Why?
4. What are some of the major issues going on in this story?
5. What are some of the keywords to focus in on?
6. Who would you have worked with first? Why?
7. What's familiar about this situation for you?
8. As a male facilitator, what would you have to be sensitive about in dealing with this situation? Why?
9. As a female facilitator, what would you have to sensitive about in dealing with this situation? Why?
10. How would you like this to all work out? Why?
11. How would you engage the group in this situation?

Lee Mun Wah's Thoughts:

My initial thoughts were that I may have overstated the goals of the workshop without accompanying them with some precautionary statements. But, like all hindsights, I was left to deal with what I had at hand. When Eve left the room I was stunned, as was the audience. I struggled with whether or not I should leave the room and go after her. My experience has taught me not to go after someone who has left the room for two reasons: One, you never know how long it will take to bring the participant back into the room. Two, a lot can happen in a room that has been traumatized, as this one apparently was. And if you aren't there – you will have missed a whole lot of valuable information about how this agency deals with conflict and a host of other issues. I call situations like these "learning moments", though at the time they don't feel that wonderful, especially if you are the facilitator and everyone is looking at you to either save them or to blame.

As I stood there for what seemed forever, I tried to survey what I had heard Eve say before she ran out as long as Ken's incendiary remarks. My first instinct was to have them both face each other. In a symbolic sense, it would be like having them both face their worst fears. Now, I wasn't sure what this might elicit in both of them, or if they would still be willing to engage, let alone move towards some resolution. I just knew that I needed more time and the present moment demanded dealing with Ken, since he was in the room and Eve wasn't (at least not physically). I also knew that I had to try to create the emotional ambiance in the room so that Eve could safely return. By "emotional ambiance," I mean an environment that is at least open to resolution and authentic dialogue.

Lee Mun Wah's Intervention:

I sent another woman who knew her to bring Eve back. I sent a woman instead of a man because a male could possibly be too threatening. I did not know if she left because he was white or because he was a man or both. While we were waiting, I told Ken that I appreciated that he told the truth, but that didn't mean it was her truth or that his truth would be received without pain or anguish. I encouraged him when Eve returned to ask her what hurt and what was familiar about what he said to her. He agreed.

When Eve returned after five minutes, I asked them both to face each other. Eve shared how most of her life, it was not just dealing with men around sexism, but white men, who felt she was a slut because she was black. Ken was shocked. He had never known this about Eve or what she had to endure as a black woman in a predominantly white male environment. I asked Ken to repeat back what Eve had shared. This was to allow Eve to be seen and heard by Ken as a person and not just as a sex object. Ken then shared how angry he was that this had happened to her.

I then asked Ken if he would have let his daughter work for a supervisor who thought the same things he had shared about women. He said absolutely not. I did this to put a "face" onto his stereotypes. I then had everyone talk about how pornography and prostitution

are promoted by seeing women as detached sex objects and certainly not as someone's daughter or mother. Ken and the men talked about how they had similar stereotypes about women that came from the media, books, advertisements and other males such as their fathers and friends. They all shared how they never really connected their images of women with their behavior. Perhaps, because they never had to, until today.

Ken apologized to Eve for his insensitivity and thanked her for being so honest. In subsequent months, they had lunch together on many occasions and became good friends. Ken wrote to me months later saying how profound the workshop had been on the rest of his life and that he had shared with his daughter what he learned about himself.

Group/Dyad Process Questions:

1. What did you learn from this experience?

2. What was the turning point for Ken? Why?

3. What was familiar about this experience for you as a woman?

4. Who did you identify with from this experience? Why or why not?

5. Where do you think Ken got his images of women from?

6. What's hard about telling the truth?

7. What have you gone through to get to this room?

8. How has racism and/or sexism affected you? In your community? At work?

Summary:

1. The importance here is not about blame, but how we have been acculturated to see each other through stereotypical images perpetuated by the media and stories we've heard in our families, in our schools, and from our friends. In addition, what are some of the images that are missing that have equally robbed us of positive, powerful representations?

2. What kept Ken from hearing Eve was not understanding her experiences as a woman in this society and the roles and privileges he has as a man that threatened her life on a daily basis.

3. The work here was for Ken to learn to ask questions of Eve instead of always keeping the issue about himself and his needs.

4. At any given moment, you can ask the people of color and the women here what their lives are like – what they have to go through on a daily basis to get to this room. The truth is always there. Saying it out loud…now that's the hard part.

I Got The Job He Wanted

A young Italian man, Tony, shared how he got a promotion over a good friend of his, Maurice, an African American. Maurice was furious because he had trained Tony and thought that he was next in line for manager. Tony kept telling his supervisor that he needed help in dealing with Maurice, but the supervisor kept telling Tony that it would all go away after awhile and not to worry – to keep reciting the company policy concerning fair practices. Maurice called the supervisor and Tony racists. He was so furious that he filed a lawsuit against the company and quit. Tony and Maurice have not talked or met since he quit a year ago. Tony shared that he has not had a peaceful night of sleep since it happened and was considering quitting. He feels horrible and blames the company and his supervisor for not giving him adequate training on how to deal with these types of situations. His whole department is still upset from what happened. Everyone has taken sides. Tony feels this situation cost him a good friend and an experienced co-worker.

Questions for the Facilitator:

1. What is coming up for you? Why?
2. What are some of the major issues in this situation?
3. What is not mentioned?
4. What are some of the key issues for Maurice?
5. What are some of the key issues for Tony?
6. How do you feel about Maurice? Why?
7. How do you feel about Tony? Why?
8. What do you think Tony should have done? Why?
9. Who would you work with first? Why?
10. How can you include the participants in your interventions?

Lee Mun Wah's Thoughts:

It was very obvious that Tony was pleading to his peers for help. There was also a statement he made about being angry at the company (specifically, the supervisor) for not training him to adequately deal with this incident with Maurice. I sensed Tony was angry at the supervisor's flippant attitude and standard company line. So along with Tony's anguish are also issues of betrayal – feeling betrayed by his supervisor and betraying his friendship with Maurice.

Along with all these issues, I kept feeling that there was this pervasive "silence" throughout what happened. Tony felt he didn't have the words to help Maurice and neither did the supervisor. Tony became the messenger of the supervisor, but somehow couldn't find his own words – and still can't. Somewhere in all of this, he needs and wants to find his voice back so that he can somehow be able to understand more clearly what he could have done about it.

I was also wondering if Tony was fulfilling another deeper fear, which was that perhaps he wasn't the best choice for manager. Or maybe even deeper, that perhaps, Maurice was. There is also the underlying accusation that remains unanswered – was the supervisor racist in his decision and was Tony a silent accomplice? Lots of issues. Now, which one to begin with?

I always try to choose the path that has the highest percentage of success and one which will serve the client and the agency as a whole in coming to grips with diversity issues. One of the easiest mistakes to make is to choose someone who is safer for us because we are scared to choose someone who is too confrontative or vocal. One of the techniques that I use when I get too scared to make a courageous choice is to remind myself that my son's life is at stake. That unless I deal with this boldly, he may face someone who is like this person and it will alter his whole life.

Lee Mun Wah's Intervention:

I asked Tony if he would be willing to role play what had happened, but he said he was too traumatized to go back there again. I had Tony choose folks in the audience that represented himself and the manager. I played the part of Maurice. When we came to the part about Maurice calling Tony a racist, I had Tony think about what he would have done differently if that happened again. He didn't know. I shared with him that he could have asked what was familiar about all of this and how it affected Maurice even today. Tony was surprised because he had never thought of something so simple. When he heard me tell Maurice's story about what black men have to go through to be considered for a job, he cried. Tony wished he could have a second try with Maurice. I told him he could. All he had to do was to call up Maurice and talk about what happened, to finish what they had begun. He agreed with a smile. I also asked the management if they would be willing to interview Maurice for any future openings and they agreed, if Maurice would be willing.

Group/Dyad Process Questions:

1.   What was familiar about this experience?

2.   Who did you identify with?

3.   What do you think Maurice wanted?

4.   How is your company/agency the same or different than what you witnessed?

5.   What did you learn about today?

Summary:

1.   What we forget is that when we have a lawsuit because of racism or sexism, we need to talk about it because it affects everyone and not just those who are involved directly. If we don't, we will never get to the source of the problem and it will remain unfinished for years to come.

2.   What is important in moments like these is to realize that we need to support the disputants rather than to take sides. We need to encourage them to talk it out and to hear each other.

3.   What we learned from this experience is the importance of asking questions so that we can learn about the life experiences that led others to this room.

4.   There is no quick fix or set way to have this dialogue. It takes patience and a willingness to stay in the room.

5.   Conflict is healthy and natural. Our silence only makes it more unsafe.

Lunchee, Lunchee!!

I rang my Tibetan bell to begin a workshop with about 100 doctors and administrative staff from a major hospital. An older doctor yelled out, "Lunchee, lunchee!!" Many in the audience laughed, but many were stunned and some looked away or down. There was a long silence. The doctor looked around quizzically.

Questions for the Facilitator:

1. What came up for you? Why?
2. What are some of the keywords to focus in on for your intervention?
3. What are some of the major issues in this vignette?
4. What are some of the issues for the older doctor? Why?
5. Who would you work with first? Why?
6. What is needed in this vignette? Why?
7. What is not being said in this vignette?

Lee Mun Wah's Thoughts:

Obviously, what happened here could be the turning point for this entire workshop. As the doctor made his comment, I kept looking around the room for reactions. There was an incredible range. No one was neutral. Now at first glance, this could be a humorous opportunity to loosen the group up or to deal with it dramatically and directly. To me, these are just some of the major choices a facilitator is faced with. I could do either one, but I first wanted to examine my motives and my fears: of questioning a doctor, of the backlash of other white participants who knew the doctor and might come to his defense, and many others.

What was seductive about this experience was that it could have been so much easier to keep my mind on my brilliant agenda and to give this incident as little attention as possible. But, something told me to look at what the purpose of this diversity workshop was all about – to look at some of the key issues that perpetuate racism – such as the denial of our own racist behaviors and attitudes. Well, here it was. The only difference was that I wasn't the one to bring it up and it wasn't on my terms or within my time frame. So much for control.

So, if in fact, one of my key goals was to get everyone involved – then here it was. The work would be what to do with all this energy – how to channel these countless reactions into a learning moment. The answer, perhaps, lay not in my knowing the outcome, but rather in acknowledging that something had happened and then lending it a voice to realize itself. There is a saying, "Where are my people so that I may lead them?" How true, how true…

Lee Mun Wah's Intervention:

I asked the doctor if he noticed what the reaction was when he said, "Lunchee, lunchee!" He said he didn't. I then asked if he'd like to know and he agreed. I then went around the whole room and asked each person to share what came up for them. That was the entire workshop. It lasted for over two hours. The responses were phenomenal and overwhelmingly emotional and truthful. The doctor eventually apologized for his insensitivity and acknowledged everyone who helped him gain a deeper insight into what he had done.

They talked about this workshop for months. It became legendary because of its powerfulness and simplicity. The truth always is.

The doctor later came to my afternoon workshop and I shared with the group what had happened previously. I then offered him my Tibetan bell as a gift. At first he was hesitant, but I told him it was not without some conditions. He was intrigued. I told him that he was never to sell this bowl, but to pass it onto his children and they, to their children, each time telling them how the bowl came into their family and why. He smiled and we both hugged as the audience applauded us.

I miss that Tibetan bowl because it took me thirty years to find and had the most beautiful sound when it rang. But, its parting was meant to be. It had found its way home and its purpose. It had served us both well.

Group/Dyad Process Questions:

1. Where do you think the doctor learned about "Lunchee, lunchee"?

2. What did you learn about what just happened?

3. What's familiar about what just happened?

4. What was good about what happened and what was hard about it?

Summary:

So often when something like this occurs, we go onto the next person or just go back to work. What that communicates is our fear to deal with conflict or anything that is emotional. What you experienced here today is what happens when we break our silence and begin to talk about what is in the middle of the room.

What is important here is that though the intentions of the good doctor may have been to be humorous, the end result was hurtful to many folks in the room. The real work here is to be willing to take responsibility and to find out why it hurt or angered some folks. It matters not how good our intentions were or if some folks weren't offended. This is not a competition over who was hurt the most; it's about being willing to hear and to acknowledge each other's separate and unique experiences and perspectives. Just because everyone doesn't have a particular painful experience, does not mean it doesn't exist or isn't traumatic for others. That is the essence of diversity – widening our worlds, and opening our eyes and hearts.

I Won't Pair Up With Him

During one of our diversity seminars, we had everyone pick someone to pair up with to talk about racism. A commotion started in the middle of the audience. A Chinese woman, May, refused to pair up with an African American man, Fred. He was visibly upset, as was she. He was furious while May kept looking away shaking her head.

I walked up to both of them and asked May if she'd be willing to share why she wouldn't pair up with Fred. She shared that she had just been mugged the previous night by a black man.

Questions for the Facilitator:

1. What came up for you? Why?
2. What are some of the major issues in this vignette?
3. What do you know about May?
4. What significance does May's cultural background play in her relationship with Fred?
5. What do you think is coming up for Fred?
6. Who would you work with first? Why?
7. What do you think Fred needs? Why?
8. What do you think May needs? Why?
9. What is hard about this vignette for you? Why?
10. In what way would you work this out between May and Fred?
11. What are some of the major obstacles in this vignette?
12. What are some of the keywords to focus in on?

Lee Mun Wah's Thoughts:

When I first heard May share her experience, I flashed back to the horror of my mother's death and the effect it had on members of our family. What enabled me to not generalize my feelings were my personal experiences with black children and their families as a Special Education teacher for 25 years in some of the poorest areas of San Francisco. Those experiences deepened my understanding of what these children and their families had to endure. I believe that it was the lack of positive experiences with African American folks that created a very insular perspective for those in my family and my other relatives, not to mention the influential racist messages and images in the media they heard everyday.

So what was needed here was not to shame May, but to have compassion and to understand her response to this painful experience. At the same time, for change to take place, what was needed was another image or experience to balance this particular traumatic event – to put it into context.

Equally important was to work with Fred, who obviously recognized this as just another racist experience to which he had become accustomed, but that continues to affect him. May and the group needed to see the impact of their generalizations on black men like Fred and the pain and anguish that they cause. In other words, to put a face to their actions and reactions and to see the impact that they have.

Who to work with first wasn't easy. To work with May might show some bias on my part as an Asian man; however, working with Fred might show some bias on my part as a male. Not an easy call. Perhaps the answer lay in working with May and Fred, but to be sure to keep the focus on May, since she was the primary speaker.

Lee Mun Wah's Intervention:

I shared with May that I knew that it would not be easy, but asked if she would be willing to share what happened to her on that night and how it affected her. She could tell by the gentleness in my voice that I cared about her and so she opened up and shared how traumatic that night had been, and how it had shaken her capacity to be open and trusting. Fred was visibly moved by what she was sharing. I then asked Fred to repeat back what he had heard and he agreed.

I asked Fred to share what was familiar about this story and what hurt him about it. He did and May intently listened to him, occasionally looking up at him. I told the audience that this is what happens when we don't have relationships with folks outside of our own; we become afraid or cautious of each other. And then one day when something does happen that is negative, we identify the whole group with that one experience. As a consequence, I told the audience that unless May met a kind and understanding black man, she would tell her children and family, and one more generation would be afraid of and angry at all black people.

An African American woman came up and shared that she would like May to come and meet her family. A number of the black men in the audience shared that they would like to begin a conversation with her, too. May agreed and started to cry. The African American woman hugged her and they cried in each other's arms as Fred touched May's shoulder and she shook his hand. The audience applauded and cried with them. I then asked the rest of the audience if they'd like to meet Fred and May, and lots of folks came down and surrounded the two of them. I told the audience that this is what community is all about – not just numbers and occasions such as diversity months, but real live relationships and friendships. And like all real live relationships, getting through the hard times and difficult times, too.

Group/Dyad Process Questions:

1. What did you learn about what happened?

2. What was familiar about what happened?

3. What kinds of stereotypes or experiences do you carry that affect how you relate or don't relate to other ethnicities?

Summary:

We are all betrayed at some time in our lives. It is what we do from that moment on that determines the direction of our lives.

So often we rely on what others or the media have told us about another ethnic group or culture. The only way we will ever have an accurate understanding is to get to know each other by entering into relationships.

Part of the problem is that people of color are often seen as a group, while whites demand to be seen as individuals. That is part of what privilege is all about – to be able to define yourself and others.

It is important to imagine what would have happened if May had not met these other folks – another generation of her family still fearful of black folks. Imagine if Fred had not paired up with May, then he would never have had a chance to share what has happened to him as a black man.

I also want you to notice what happened when we didn't take sides, but supported each person to be heard and valued. Each felt heard and respected. Now that is what community is all about.

I'm Afraid of Harlem

I was facilitating a group of high school students throughout New York and one Asian student, Elliot, stood up and said he was afraid of going into Harlem because he had heard it was dangerous. A number of black students were upset with his comments. A number of the Asian students looked down on the floor and away from the group.

Questions for the Facilitator:

1. What came up for you? Why?
2. What do you think was coming up for the Asian and African American students?
3. What do you think are some of Elliot's issues?
4. What is sitting in the middle of the room?
5. How would you deal with the African American students? Why?
6. How would you deal with the Asian students? Why?
7. What do you think the African American students need? Why?
8. What do you think Elliot is asking for?
9. What are some of the keywords to focus in on?
10. Who would you work with first? Why?

Lee Mun Wah's Thoughts:

Elliot revealed his fears about going to Harlem because of his stereotypes – perhaps from stories he'd heard from family members or friends. In some ways, I had a sense he was also saying, "I'd go, if only…." So the underlying request might be that he'd like to go under the right circumstances. I also felt that he needed to meet some of the folks he was told to be afraid of – African Americans. The audience was filled with other African American folks, some whose facial expressions led me to believe they possibly lived in or had visited Harlem.

I felt that the folks from Harlem could possibly provide a face and a voice for Elliot to experience and relate to. Not much different than what we all want for ourselves – to be seen and appreciated and related to in a personal and real way. I also viewed Elliot's response and honesty as an opening to allow others to share their own stereotypes as well.

Lee Mun Wah's Intervention:

I had all the students who either visited Harlem or lived there, to come down and share with Elliot what they loved about living there and what it was really like. Afterwards, I asked Elliot if he'd be willing to let some of these students show him the real Harlem. He agreed with a smile, as well as a number of other Asian students who wanted to go along. Within minutes, even the white students wanted to go.

Group/Dyad Process Questions:

1. What was familiar about what happened?

2. What have you heard about certain areas and how did that affect your behavior and perceptions of those folks who lived there? Where do you think those fears came from?

3. What moved you about what happened here?

4. What did it take for Elliot to change his mind about visiting Harlem?

Summary:

1. We all stereotype people and don't talk about it, but as long as we remain silent, our stereotyping keep us from truly getting to know others who are different from ourselves.

2. To break through our stereotypes we need to engage in a conversation and to develop a relationship with each other that is honest and open to mutual understanding.

I'm Leaving This Town

A European American woman in a wheelchair, named Tina, shared how she was raped by a Palestinian man on a date and was leaving town as soon as she could because it so traumatized her. She was crying and visibly trembling. She said that since then she has been frightened of all Middle Eastern men.

Questions for the Facilitator:

1. What came up for you about this vignette?
2. What didn't she say?
3. What are some of the keywords in this story?
4. What are some of Tina's issues?
5. What is Tina trying to say to the group? Why?
6. What is hard about this vignette? Why?
7. What does Tina need?
8. Who do you work with first? The audience or Tina?
9. How can you incorporate the audience?
10. Who are you looking for in this audience? Why?
11. What do you think will change Tina's mind about leaving? Why?

Lee Mun Wah's Thoughts:

I'm not quite sure why I wondered how she got paralyzed, except that there was something in the ease with which she expressed herself that made me wonder if she had ever been able-bodied. (Ah, one more stereotype about physically challenged folks). In short, I wanted to know the historical context of her journey to get to this place in time.

Her conclusion that all Palestinian men were dangerous due to being raped by one man of color exemplified how this society often generalizes about people of color from the actions of one individual. I wanted to find a way for her to come to this realization on her own and to explore where it came from and how it continues to affect her perceptions of people of color.

I also thought that I needed to validate the trauma of her rape because it could be so easy to dismiss her response as simply being racist.

Another consciousness that I brought to this vignette was the impact of my being a person of color. I was wondering what impact my being Asian and a man would have on her willingness to also be open. And so I became aware of the space between us and her response to me. I kept watching her eyes and facial expressions as she spoke to me. In moments like this, voice tone and facial expressions are critical. I took my cues from her and acted accordingly.

Throughout her telling her story, I kept looking at the audience for someone of Palestinian heritage who might be reacting to what she was saying. At the same time, I was also looking for a woman of EuroAmerican heritage who Tina might be able to relate to and trust.

Lee Mun Wah's Intervention:

I asked her how she came to be in a wheelchair and she shared that her former husband, who was also white, threw her against a wall in a fit of alcoholic rage, leaving her paralyzed from the waist down. I asked her if she was now afraid of all white men. She was surprised at my statement and shared with the audience, "No, I wasn't. This is the first time I've ever thought of him or myself for that matter, as coming from a white group. I have to really think about that. I just saw him as a person – an individual."

A couple shared that they were Palestinian and that they were sorry that she was raped and that there were also kind and respectful Palestinians, too. They said that they'd like to invite her over for dinner. She cried and said she'd like that. They all hugged and the audience was stunned. There wasn't a dry eye in the entire room. This is quite typical in most of my workshops. I think perhaps because so much has been kept inside for so many people of color and women, that the release of all those years of anguish and pain is a huge relief because they are finally acknowledged and validated for what they went through.

Group/Dyad Process Questions:

1. What was the turning point for Tina?

2. Who did you identify with? Why?

3. What was hard and what was good about this experience?

4. What did you learn from this experience?

5. Which groups are you afraid of and where did that fear come from?

Summary:

1. It is not easy to revisit our past, especially if it is traumatic. I want to thank Tina for taking that journey. Sometimes if we don't, a part of us remains there – unfinished and forever frozen with fear and doubt. I also want to thank those who came forth and took a risk to stand with her by opening their homes and sharing their world with her. That is what it will take if we are ever to end racism and all the other isms – to walk each other home.

2. What you saw here today was not easy. There was no script for this, except to begin. Each person here had no idea what they were going to say today. But, it is my belief that what happened was no accident. Someone once said that there are no coincidences – just planned accidents waiting to happen. I believe that these folks met today because they needed each other – they just didn't know how much.

3. I also want to thank each of you who witnessed this. I hope that it will inspire you to walk across the room like you did today and to get to know this person you paired up with. Visit their homes and open your doors to each other – who knows – you might have a great dinner and possibly a new friendship.

4. When I think about what "community" really means to me…it is taking care of each other like a family should. When we do that as neighbors and as friends, then we will grow as a community and as a nation.

My Father Was A Nazi

This particular incident occurred at a University at which I was showing *The Color of Fear* to an audience of about 300 students. After the film, we had folks come up to talk about their reactions. A young man, Frank, came up and shared with the audience that his father was a Nazi during the war and that he felt horrible about their family legacy of racism and participation in the Holocaust. During the entire time Frank was talking, he kept looking down and crying, trying hard not to look at the audience.

Questions for the Facilitator:

1. What is coming up for you about this situation?
2. What are some major issues here?
3. How do you feel about Frank? His father?
4. What do you think Frank wants? What do you think he needs?
5. Who would you work with first – the group or Frank? Why?
6. What kind of intervention would you use? Why?
7. If you worked with Frank, what would be some good questions to ask him?
8. If you worked with the audience, what would be some good questions to ask them?
9. What are some of the keywords that gave you clues about Frank? How could you use those keywords to aid you in the development of your intervention strategy?

Lee Mun Wah Thoughts:

There are many issues here – the foremost being shame. Therapeutically, the face of shame is one of looking away. The difference between shame and guilt is that the guilty person feels badly for a particular act or situation, whereas the shamed person feels that they *are* shameful. The work, then, is to help participants come to forgive themselves and to become a part of the community again. This is not an easy task, since an aspect of shame is the feeling of being rightfully punished and isolated.

There is also another step that is important in breaking the cycle of shame. So often, shame is perpetuated by the escalating fears of what others might be feeling towards them. This perpetuation of silence from both parties only adds to the cycle of shame. So it is essential to break the silence between them.

Lee Mun Wah's Intervention:

When I realized he was experiencing an issue with shame, I asked him to look up and to look around the room and to make eye contact with the audience. I did this because he was avoiding having to look at them, which only added to his perceived shame. Then I requested that Frank ask certain folks in the audience what they thought of him, now that he had shared that his father was a Nazi soldier. I did this not only to involve the audience, but to get at his worst fears of negative judgment.

I told Frank that I knew that this would not be easy, but that it was important to bring his fears into the present tense so that he could get on with his life. I said this to let him know that I wanted to help him find a way to reckon with his past and to let him know I cared. He agreed and began to ask to hear from certain members of the audience. I then asked the audience if they would be willing to tell him the truth and they all raised their hands. I did this to put a face to the audience and to assure Frank of their sincerity and their willingness to share their perception of him. This was a way to break the wall of silence that he had built around himself.

One by one, each person told him how moved they were by his story and that he wasn't responsible for his father's actions. He cried as each person shared with him how they felt towards him. Some even talked about how they, too, had gone through similar situations of shame with other family members' attitudes and behaviors – particularly those from Southern families or ones that were extremely prejudiced.

After this experience, Frank shared with the audience how he had kept this secret inside of himself all these many years and that today he was finally able to let go of the heavy responsibility of carrying his father's shame. He also shared how much fear he had that folks in the audience would feel disdain for him and his family and how relieved and surprised he felt that people actually felt closer towards him and more trusting because of his sincerity.

One added note: If there had been any folks of Jewish heritage or religion, I would have asked them to share what came up for them in hearing Frank's story. Though this might have been painful for the Jewish folks, it might also have afforded them an opportunity to tell Frank what they needed from him as an ally of those who endured the Holocaust or who had family members that were in the camps. There is a Jewish motto in New York on one of the museum walls: "Lest we forget." Frank's memory of his father's involvement is important to keep alive so that the horror and inhumanity of what happened will not be allowed to occur again. It is true that those who do not remember history are bound to have it repeated.

Group/Dyad Process Questions:

1. What came up for you in watching this?

2. How did you feel about Frank? Why?

3. Was any of this familiar? Why?

4. What did you learn from all of this?

Summary:

1. Every culture and every nation has a history of brutality and injustice, but that doesn't mean that there weren't also great inventors and writers, artists, leaders and freedom fighters. What is important here is to always remember how our actions can harm and destroy the lives of others and to see that it never happens again to any one.

2. I want to thank Frank for his honesty and wiliness to share how he felt. Perhaps, what he reminded each of us was to remember to not only forgive others, but also ourselves. Someone once said that guilt is really coagulated grief. To break that cycle of paralyzing grief, we need to talk about our experiences and our fears, as well as what we need in order to move on with our lives.

My Name Is George

This workshop occurred at a diversity conference in Canada. A Canadian Indian man, George, shared how he had lived here for many years as a child. He said that growing up, many folks stared at him and that he often felt alone and an outsider. I asked him how he got his name George. He told the audience that the Catholic missionaries had given him that name.

Questions for the Facilitator:

1. What came up for you in this vignette?
2. What are some of the keywords?
3. What are some of the issues that George is facing in this community?
4. What isn't being said here?
5. What's a good set of questions to ask George? Why?
6. Who would you work with first? Why?
7. What does George need? Why?
8. What would be a good set of questions to ask the audience? Why?

Lee Mun Wah's Thoughts:

Asking George if that was his Native name is a standard question I ask of persons of color to illustrate the effects of racism. What struck me was that he was baptized Catholic and that a priest had renamed him. Something wasn't being said here and I was curious, so I pursued him with more questions.

What I discovered during this process was how thoughtfully and honestly George answered all my questions. He seemed to sense that I was going somewhere that he already suspected, but hadn't put into words for fear of what it might mean. I think that sometimes we accept our silence because we don't know what to do with the truth and are afraid of how it will affect us.

Lee Mun Wah's Intervention:

I asked George what his real name was. He told the audience. I then asked him why his name was changed to George. He said that the missionaries told him that he was a savage and needed a Christian name.

I then asked the audience to raise their hands if they were baptized Catholic. I asked how many had their names changed? Only the people of color had their hands left up. I asked why were only the people of color considered "savages"? Why weren't the whites? From here, the folks of color shared story after story about the two Americas – one for whites and the other for people of color – one 'civilized', the other 'savage'.

Group/Dyad Process Questions:

1. What came up for you?

2. How did you feel about George? Why?

3. What moved you about what happened?

4. What was good and what was hard about all of this?

5. What was familiar to you about what happened? Why?

6. Do you think name changes are still going on? Why or why not?

7. Is what happened to George symbolic of other differences in this society? Give examples.

Summary:

1. As you can see, there are two Americas, and they are painfully difficult for some folks and not so for others. The work here is to see that no one has to go through something like this simply because of the color of their skin.

2. Often we think that it is the Ku Klux Klan or some skinhead that is racist, but racism is alive and well on every street in this country – in our corporations, schools, churches and social agencies. The real work is not who to blame, but rather to look at ourselves and to take responsibility for our actions. Buddhists say "We do not learn from experience, but rather from our willingness to experience."

3. As you can see from what came up as George was telling his story, at any given moment we can ask a question if we truly want to find out the life stories of those who are different from ourselves. The real test is whether we are willing to hear the truth. Do we truly want to know the truth?

4. Each of you paired up with someone today. You can, if you choose, get to know them. The real test of any community that desires multiculturalism is whether or not they will allow that diversity into their workplaces, into their churches and places of worship, and into their friendships. You see, true diversity is not on a shiny brochure or an occasional celebration – it is and has always been, our willingness to live it, practice it, and honor it in all aspects of our lives.

Tell Him, Tom!

We had just shown the film, *The Color of Fear*, for a government agency in California. We were meeting with their diversity council, and the head of the department had to make a final decision to roll out the program for all the employees. The supervisor, Fred, asked each of the individual members to share their thoughts of the workshop and whether or not they should roll it out to the entire agency. All of the members of the diversity council were folks of color with the exception of two white males, Barry and Tom. All of the folks of color and Tom felt the workshop was a tremendous success and recommended it for all of the agency. When we came to the last white male, Barry, he shared that he had reservations about the workshop because he thought it might bring up too many emotions and would upset some folks.

The supervisor then decided that obviously there was too much controversy surrounding this film and that they shouldn't roll it out to the rest of the agency. Everyone was shocked. Fred was called out the room for an important phone call. The room was silent as they waited for him to come back. Tom was very upset and still reeling in disbelief. Barry continued reading his set of papers.

Questions for the Facilitator:

1. What came up for you? Why?
2. What are some of the keywords in this vignette?
3. What are some of the key issues sitting in the room?
4. Why do you think Fred responded in the way he did towards Barry?
5. Why do you think Tom was in disbelief?
6. What is needed here? Why?
7. What is difficult about this situation? Why?
8. Who would you begin with? Why?
9. Who would you not go to? Why?
10. How do you want this to all turn out? How will you get there?

Lee Mun Wah's Thoughts:

I was shocked by the supervisor's cursory conclusion that the workshop was obviously too controversial despite the overwhelming support that had been voiced. It was apparent that Barry, as a white man, was given much more credence and power than the folks of color. Somehow, a part of me realized how familiar this all was, and yet another part has never gotten over how much racism still exists and how much it hurts me each time it happens.

In the process, I noticed how shocked Tom was at Fred's response. Somehow, I sensed I needed to get Tom involved in the decision-making process. I had talked with Tom earlier and appreciated that his heart was in the right place about diversity. Barry, on the other hand was distant and arrogantly silent during the workshop.

Lee Mun Wah's Intervention:

I told Tom to speak in a strong tone and to tell Fred when he returned, "Fred, we're going to do this workshop." Tom was surprised and curious as to why I made such a strange request. I told him, "Just trust me." When Fred returned, Tom said for him to do the workshop. Fred looked at him and nodded, "Okay."

Group/Dyad Process Questions:

1. What came up for you about this experience?

2. Were you surprised or not surprised? Why?

3. What was familiar about this to you?

4. Why do you think the supervisor didn't acknowledge the people of color's reactions?

5. Why did you think the supervisor listened to Tom?

6. What was good about this and what was hard for you? Why?

Summary:

1.   Sometimes we are unconscious about who we hear and who we do not, who we see and who we do not see. The work here is not just for the person who is unconscious, but also for those who witnessed what happened and whether they will speak up. Martin Luther King Jr. once said, "When all is done, what will be remembered is not the words of our enemies, but the silence of our friends."

2.   There are two Americas, and today we had a glimpse into that division: the difference in perception and privilege. We need to talk about the problems we have, our silence, and how our looking down will not make them go away. Before we can end racism or sexism or any other isms, we first need to acknowledge that there is a problem and to ask ourselves what part we play and what we are willing to do about it.

The Car Repair

I asked a group if there were ever any stories about racism that they had kept secret and a young African American woman, Jenn, raised her hand. She shared how she went to an auto repair shop with her co-worker, Margaret, because her brakes needed work. When they got there, the head of the shop only talked to Margaret, who was white, about the car. Jenn was very hurt at being ignored by the mechanic and Margaret.

An older African American woman, Linda, and another older African American man, Thomas, yelled at Jenn for not being assertive enough. "Girl," Linda said, "you don't let something like that happen to you! Don't let no white woman do that to you. She doesn't care about you. You gotta take care of yourself!" Margaret protested under her breath, "Yes, I do… I was just trying to help her." Looking down and afraid, Jenn said, "I know you do…"

Questions for the Facilitator:

1. What came up for you in reading this vignette?
2. What are some of the keywords to focus in on?
3. Why do you think the mechanic ignored Jenn?
4. Why do you think Margaret didn't say anything to the mechanic?
5. What did Jenn need from Margaret? Why?
6. What is familiar about this scenario?
7. Why do you think Linda and Thomas were so angry at Jenn?
8. What does Jenn need in this situation? Why?
9. Who would you work with first? Why?
10. How would you work with the audience?
11. What is not being said here?
12. What is difficult about this scenario? Why?

Lee Mun Wah's Thoughts:

This was not going to be an easy situation because of all the folks involved and the many emotions being expressed. Yet, there were signs everywhere that beginning with Linda was the obvious choice. When I looked at Jenn, I realized that she needed to express her anger and to get back her own voice. My hesitation with working with her was that her demeanor showed me she was going further and further into herself. If I chose Margaret, I would be duplicating what had happened at the car repair. I also didn't choose the African American man for that same reason – yet another man taking over the conversation and having the power to choose and define the issue.

Somehow I sensed that there was a link between Linda and Jenn. Perhaps a younger Linda being reflected in Jenn. It was the intensity of Linda's response that told me that something was still unfinished in her life – perhaps she was speaking to that anguish and loss in herself, as well.

Lee Mun Wah's Intervention:

I asked Linda what was familiar about what happened to Jenn. She talked about how she had to struggle with racism when she was young and that nobody was there to help her so she had to learn how to be strong on her own. I then asked her what she thought she needed years ago. She said that she wished someone was there for her. "What do you think Jenn needs?" I asked.

Linda smiled back at me, "Perhaps, what I needed…" With that Jenn started crying. I told Linda to go over to her, "I think she needs you right now." They cried in each other's arms.

But it wasn't Jenn that Linda was yelling at, it was herself and the injustice in her life. Jenn only brought her back to that place – the point of her departure – where she started protecting herself – and never allowing herself to be that vulnerable with a white person again.

In working with Jenn, I encouraged Margaret to ask Jenn what was familiar about what happened at the repair shop. This empowered Jenn and gave her a chance to deepen her relationship with Margaret – one that had never breached the subject of their ethnic differences or privileges – and a chance also to be heard and understood as a woman of color. I also asked Jenn to tell Margaret what she needed from her when faced with the situation with the mechanic.

Group/Dyad Process Questions:

1. Who did you identify with in this situation?

2. Why do you think Jenn didn't react to Margaret at the car repair?

3. What was familiar about this incident?

4. What did you learn from this exchange?

Summary:

1. You see, sometimes what we hate in others is a reflection of what we hate in ourselves. We need to avoid shaming that part of ourselves that we see in others, and to remember to acknowledge those hurt and unfinished places within us. As you can see today, at any given moment we can get a second chance in life to give to others what we didn't get. Just as a parent gets to give their children what they didn't get, Linda got to go back into that place in her life that was unfinished. Only this time, by helping Jenn, she was able to help herself, too.

2. It is so easy here to take sides in situations like these. The real work is to support everyone to be heard and to be acknowledged.

3. It's also important when someone tells us their story of being hurt and victimized, to remember to listen and to ask questions in support of them, rather than distancing them by our judgments and blaming.

I'm a Lifer

After showing one of our films, a Latino man named Luis shared about being passed over again and again for a promotion. Finally he confronted his supervisor who told him the reason was because he didn't have a B.A. degree. He went back to night school and got a B.A. in business administration. It has now been two years since his graduation and he still hasn't gotten his promotion. He says he doesn't care anymore – he is a lifer.

Questions for the Facilitator:

1. What came up for you in reading this vignette?
2. What are some of the keywords?
3. What are some of the issues that Luis is bringing up?
4. What angered Luis? Why?
5. What hurt him? Why?
6. What does Luis want?
7. What isn't Luis saying?
8. Who would you start with first? Why?
9. How would you work with the audience?

Lee Mun Wah's Thoughts:

As I was listening to Luis, I realized that he was trying to hide his disappointment over not getting the promotion. He seemed resigned to his fate and determined not to show his emotions. I sensed that he was just a step away from getting angry and revealing how hurt he truly was. In many ways, I sensed he was also suppressing his feelings of betrayal and of being duped.

I also knew from the frankness of his story that he appreciated directness. He was a survivor, but he was also someone who had been deeply hurt and was still feeling unfinished. I needed to be tender but honest with him to gain his trust. My physical and emotional demeanor needed to be respectful and caring. Trust was utmost in this exchange.

Lee Mun Wah's Intervention:

I asked Luis what a "lifer" meant for him and he said that it was an employee whose body was here, but nothing else – waiting for his time to be up so he could retire. I told him that this was the first time I had ever heard that term and that I was saddened by it. I wondered if anyone else knew that he felt that way. I then asked if anyone also felt that way themselves. A lot of hands were raised and many were nodding their heads in agreement. Most of the administrators were shocked. I put my hand on Luis' shoulder and told him that I heard him say he didn't care, but that somehow I wasn't convinced. I sensed what he was really saying, "You aren't going to hurt me anymore". His eyes moistened and he nodded.

I then asked if the company would consider re-evaluating his application for promotion and they agreed. Luis was deeply moved and appreciative. He said, "All I wanted was an opportunity. No handouts, just a chance to show I was qualified."

Group/Dyad Process Questions:

1. What were you like on your first day here and what are you like now?
    What happened and how does it affect you today?

2. What do you need from this company/agency to feel valued and supported?

3. What does a company/agency lose when you are not valued or rewarded?

4. What do you think Luis lost? Why?

Summary:

1. I hoped what you learned today was how easily we can find out about another person by simply asking them a deeper, more personal question.

2. What we learned today was how much a company loses when someone feels like a "lifer" – they feel powerless, less creative or energetic, and less involved. Everyone loses. Imagine all this "human resource" that is wasted and how it could have benefitted everyone, including the company.

3. Seventy percent of all promotions today is still based on who someone knows in a company. Companies need to take notice of how racism and sexism affect their decisions and promotions. When a community looks at its top 100 executives in a company – it should reflect what is represented in its community as well as what is on their shiny brochures touting diversity.

The best recruitment for any company are the folks who work for you. When they feel valued, acknowledged and challenged – imagine how great a company this will be.

Who's Going To Stand Up?

An African American man, Elliot, shared how he was so tired of never seeing white folks stand up against racism/sexism. I asked the group to please stand if they would be willing to stand up against sexism. Everyone did, except one EuroAmerican man. When I asked the group who would stand up against racism, once again everyone did, except the same white man named Sam. Elliot was furious, he yelled out at Sam, "See what I mean? How come you aren't standing? Say something!" Sam looked down, turning his chair away from Elliot. The room was dead silent for what seemed like minutes.

Questions for the Facilitator:

1. What came up for you reading this vignette?
2. What are some of the keywords?
3. What angered Elliot? Why?
4. What is familiar about Elliot's frustration?
5. What is Elliot saying he needs and wants from EuroAmericans? Why?
6. What came up for you about Sam? Why?
7. Were Elliot's accusations of Sam justified? Why or why not?
8. Who would you work with first? Why?
9. What are the major issues here?
10. How would you include the group?

Lee Mun Wah's Thoughts:

There were obviously a lot of emotions going on in the room. Sometimes it is easy to become frightened by the chaos and volume of voices and miss the pain and anguish that is being expressed. As I was watching Elliot, I kept thinking of how liberating it must have been for him to finally express himself, and yet at the same time, how frightening, too, because of the possible consequences. What Elliot was doing required a whole lot of risk taking.

There was a point, too, when I wondered if Elliot trusted what he was seeing, particularly when all the white participants stood up. I kept wondering if he thought they stood because of peer pressure or their fear of an angry black man. When Sam didn't stand, though it was puzzling, there was a sense of relief in the room – like an opening to something more real and direct and deep was going to take place.

I knew by Sam's body language that this was not just a matter of defiance. His face and depressed body language spoke to a deeper story. The trick would be how to acknowledge Elliot and still be able to help Sam feel safe enough to open up. This would take a lot of diplomacy and some good old-fashioned luck. I sensed that the opening lay in Sam's journey of getting to this room. It had little to do with Elliot and everything to do with him, if Sam were to heal. My work would be to become a bridge for the two of them – an entrance into the past.

Lee Mun Wah's Intervention:

I asked Elliot to tell Sam why he was so angry with him and what was familiar about this scenario. I then sat next to Sam. I put my hand on his shoulder and told him that I knew this wasn't easy. But, I had a question that I was wondering about. I asked him what was familiar about this scenario with Elliot. Sam waited for a moment and then shared in a very quiet voice that his father was an alcoholic, and that he and his brother often hid and kept real quiet, because if he found them he would beat them in a furious rage. I asked him how those experiences in his family affected him today, and he said, "I guess I'm still running and hiding."

I then asked the group if they knew these things about Elliot or Sam and no one raised their hands. I then proceeded to share with the group that both of these men would need their support in the days and months ahead. That Elliot had shared he needed folks to stand up for him against racism and sexism and that Sam needed to know that he didn't need to run away or to hide anymore. That he could speak up and not be harmed or abused. The group wholeheartedly raised their hands in a show of support. Elliot walked across the room and hugged Sam. Sobbing, Elliot said, "I am so sorry, I just didn't know." Sam said to the group and Elliot, "And I guess what I need to do is take a chance again."

Group/Dyad Process Questions:

1. What came up for you during this experience?

2. Who did you identify with? Why?

3. What was good about this experience and what was hard about it?

4. Why do you think Elliot was so angry?

5. What's familiar about this experience for you?

6. Have you ever not stood up against something you knew was wrong? Why?

Summary:

1. What we can see here today is that everyone has a story. Sometimes it's easier to make assumptions because of someone's silence or anger. But, behind each of those emotions is a journey that begs for compassion and understanding. We have only to ask and to be willing to listen and try to understand.

2. What Elliot asked for was for someone to stand up. It took a lot of courage and risk taking for him to share his pain and anguish today. This company and community are lucky to have someone so brave and courageous. I was also touched by his reaching out to Sam and taking responsibility for his assumptions.

3. I also want us to remember the words that Sam shared with us, too. That given all that has happened to him, maybe it is time to stop running. He might be able to do that now that he has shared his story.

4. All that Elliot and Sam wanted were to be treated kindly and justly. That is a world worth standing up for and fighting for – a just and equitable world for ourselves and our children. Perhaps, that is the secret to world peace – taking care of each other, one person at a time.

We Just Love Mary

Mary was an African American administrator at a major University. During the workshop she talked about how much she loved working there and was looking forward to her retirement and spending more time with her grandson. She also lamented about how her eight year old grandson was experiencing racism from his teachers and how angry she was about this, because he was so bright and enthusiastic about school when he first started.

She also talked about how few people of color were there when she first started compared with how many were here now. When she was finished, her colleagues gave her a standing ovation. However, I noticed that her black colleagues, particularly the black males who were all sitting together, looked away or downward and did not applaud. No one else seemed to notice.

Questions for the Facilitator:

1. What came up for you about Mary's story?
2. What are the issues sitting in the middle of the room?
3. What are a few keywords by Mary that gives some clues about the issues facing this institution?
4. What comes up for you about her black colleagues? Why do you think they didn't applaud?
5. How can you use what Mary has said to help you with your intervention?
6. What do your instincts tell you about where to go next? Why?
7. How did you react to the standing ovation? Why?
8. What came up for you about Mary's grandson? Why?
9. How many incidents of intent and impact did you notice?

Lee Mun Wah's Thoughts:

On the surface all seems well on the ranch, but there are some disturbing insinuations. Why did her black colleagues not applaud? Why were they sitting away from the group and all together? What was Mary's relationship with them?

Experience tells me that there was a story underneath all of the applause. Mary was obviously the most tenured black member at the University. She probably came to the school at a time when the school was probably mostly white. She may have had to endure a great deal of racism and isolation.

Like so many of her generation, she carried the burden of being a torchbearer. What was the cost? What was the trade-off? What did she endure to survive? How did she assimilate? What kinds of messages did she get from her white colleagues?

The lack of applause from her black colleagues also caught my attention, as well as their sitting amongst themselves. There seemed to be two worlds operating in the room, with Mary being the lone representative for the blacks, playing the middle role – perhaps caught between two worlds.

Though it was seductive to focus on her black colleagues in the room, I was unsure if the room was safe enough for them to speak the truth. Something told me that fear was in the air – thick and familiar. If I had not yet won their approval or trust, it would be a risky venture to expect their willingness to tell the truth so easily, especially to a stranger who was leaving at the end of the workshop.

Perhaps, the answer lay in what Mary didn't say.

Lee Mun Wah's Intervention:

It occurred to me that one of the ways to kill an undesirable message is to kill the messenger or to only see what you want to see. With that in mind, I asked the audience to share what they heard Mary say. One by one, each of her white colleagues shared the parts of her story that most moved them. As each was sharing, I noticed that Mary changed from feeling pleasantly listened to, to someone who became increasingly upset.

When I asked her what she noticed about the responses, she looked at me and then to the audience and said, "What I noticed was that everyone chose only the positive things I said, but nothing about how I felt about my grandson." She looked at her black colleagues and told them that it wasn't until today that she realized how much she had been acculturated by whites to mold herself to fit their definitions of who they wanted her to be, remembering on many occasions being told, "I am so glad you're not like them". "Well, today," she said, "I want to tell especially my black brothers and sisters – I am you. And I want to tell you how sad I am to realize that it took almost the end of my career to discover how I have isolated and blamed you for not assimilating the way that I had. I am so sorry." With that, her black colleagues applauded her with tears in their eyes. One

young black professor shared how he was labeled as a troublemaker for speaking up about the racism at this institution and how he felt so alone and attacked after he spoke up. He also said that he had looked to Mary to say something, but she never did. Mary told him how sorry she was for not being there and he nodded with tears in his eyes.

I then asked her white colleagues to share how they felt. Many talked about not realizing how they had made Mary into someone they wanted her to be – white, always positive and caring, but never angry or hurt and never "too black."

Group/Dyad Process Questions:

1. What part of this discussion moved you? What upset you? Why?
2. What do you leave at the door? How does that affect you?
3. What do you lose when folks like Mary leave a part of themselves at the door?
4. What were you like when you first came here and what are you like now?
5. What has society taught you about people of color when they get angry?
6. What are the consequences for people of color in showing their whole selves?
7. What has it taken for you to get to this room?
8. What do you need/want from the folks in this room?
9. What don't you want from the folks in this room?
10. What will it take for you to feel fully appreciated and valued?

Summary Points:

1. Acknowledge the courage it took for Mary to tell the truth and to take responsibility for her actions or inaction.

2. Thank the group for their honesty and willingness to tell the truth about their part in this experience.

3. Encourage the participants to ask each other if they feel supported or unsupported here at this institution and to be willing to hear and believe the answers.

4. Encourage the participants to meet with each other on a daily basis and to ask each other questions, not because there is a crisis, but because it is important.

5. Share how, despite their good intentions, the impact of their words and actions affected lots of folks.

6. Practice becoming more aware of people's reactions and to be willing to stop and ask what just happened.

Martin Luther King Jr. once said, "What will be remembered are not the words of our enemies, but the silence of our friends."

My Name Was Changed

A young Vietnamese man, Thuy, shared how his name was changed by a teacher because she felt he should have an American name now that he was no longer in his native country. A Latina woman, Maria, told the group that she knew exactly what he was talking about because her co-workers changed her name from Maria to Mary. They said it was easier to pronounce and because she needed an "American" name, too.

A EuroAmerican woman, Debbie, stood up and said that she was fed up with the way this was all going. She said that she couldn't understand why it was such a big deal having to change names. "I was called Debbie and my name was Deborah. So what? It's just a name…"

Questions for the Facilitator:

1. What came up for you about this vignette?
2. What are some of the keywords to focus in on?
3. What do Thuy and Maria have in common? Why?
4. Why do you think Debbie is upset?
5. What is not being said?
6. What is Maria saying about being an "American"?
7. What do Thuy and Maria want or need? Why?
8. What is Debbie asking of Thuy and Maria? Why?
9. Who would you work with first? Why?
10. How would you include the group?
11. What's hard about this vignette?

Lee Mun Wah's Thoughts:

What was essential here was to keep my eyes on the reactions of the people of color, Maria and Thuy, as well as the rest of the audience. It would have been very seductive to have just answered Debbie's question as a facilitator, but having Maria or Thuy answer would allow them to finally respond in a way that they couldn't when they were younger.

What Debbie shared had larger implications and a deeper significance than just a harmless question. The implication is that Debbie doesn't have this pain, so why should you? In other words, you are the same as she is or could be. The deeper significance is that Debbie feels that way because, like most white folks, she sees herself not as a member of an ethnic group, but as an individual. She has overcome racism or prejudice and so should people of color. You see, her success from her point of view has nothing to do with race, but rather from a personality or life change such as a name or a change of hair color or speaking better English. She does not see the racial implications for Maria and Thuy, because it has not been a daily issue in her life.

Debbie reminds me of a EuroAmerican woman on Oprah who said, "All my life I have been taught that I am what is considered normal. What that means is that if I am normal, then everyone else is below me."

Lee Mun Wah's Intervention:

I acknowledged hearing Debbie say that she didn't mind having her name changed. But, I also heard her ask a question and answer it at the same time. I heard her ask what "the big deal" was all about? I told her that if she wanted to know why it was such a "big deal," then would she be willing to ask Thuy and Maria? She did.

Maria shared how angry her parents felt when she changed her name to Mary because Maria was their grandmother's name. Maria was afraid to say something because the teacher also laughed along with the other children who couldn't pronounce it. She wanted to blend in, so she let the teacher change it, but felt that it wasn't fair because the other white children didn't have to change their names. Thuy also said that this was exactly what happened for him, too. The result was that he still doesn't feel like a part of the community even today.

When I asked them why it was important to keep their real names, they each said that it was a part of them – a part of their family traditions. That even though they were now American citizens, their names were a way of paying respect to their ancestors who had helped them get here.

I then asked how many others had their names changed, too, and gave them time to share their experiences and the effect it had on their lives. Debbie kept nodding throughout each story, indicating that she believed them.

Group/Dyad Process Questions:

1. What came up for you during this experience?

2. What was familiar?

3. Have you ever had your name changed? Why?

4. Who did you identify with? Why?

5. What was hard about this experience for you?

6. Who is an "American"? Who is not?

7. Did you believe Maria and Thuy? Why or why not?

8. Is Debbie familiar? In what ways?

Summary:

1. Just because something feels good to us, doesn't mean it is good for everyone else.

2. We need to learn how to ask someone questions if we want to learn what is important to them. There is a saying, "Love thy neighbor as thyself." But I think it is really, "Love thy neighbor as they would like to be loved."

3. We need to learn to listen and not just see the world through our own eyes. It is a whole lot like fish, who think that the whole world is water. Until one day when they are caught, they realize how large the world really is.

4. I want to thank Thuy and Maria for so courageously sharing their stories and to Debbie, who was bold enough to ask why and to also be open to hearing the truth.

There's No Glass Ceiling Here!

A young woman, Sarah, shared how she felt there was a glass ceiling for women here at this college. Tom, a fellow employee, yelled out, "Oh come on, Sarah, there is not a glass ceiling here at this college! Any woman, if she has the skills, can rise up to be a secretary here." The women in the room were visibly upset, with lots of hands raised demanding to respond to him. A white man in the front row rolled his eyes and looked away from Tom.

Questions for the Facilitator:

1. What came up for you in reading this vignette? Why?
2. What were the keywords?
3. What do you think Sarah is feeling? Why?
4. What do you think Tom is feeling? Why?
5. What are the key issues in this situation?
6. What does Sarah need? Why?
7. What does Tom need? Why?
8. Who would you go to first? Why?
9. How would you include the group in this conversation?
10. How do intent and impact become important issues in this situation?
11. What are some considerations for a facilitator around gender issues?
12. What is not being said here by Tom and Sarah?
13. What's familiar about this situation? Why?
14. What are some clues as to where to go?

Lee Mun Wah's Thoughts:

Something told me from the beginning that this wasn't as easy as it looked – just calling on the other women to speak to their outrage about what he said. There were other reactions – from the man in the front who looked away and the defensiveness of Tom. Tom, in particular, was defending someone or something. My hunch was that it was himself, which was why he was adamant in his reactions to Sarah's comments.

Often we react to comments because we think they are talking about us, when, in fact, they may be referring to a group or to others generally. In this case, my sense was that Tom was wondering if Sarah was thinking that about him. What happened was useful as a catalyst, because it revealed Tom's sexism, which before may have been hidden or not vocalized.

I was uncertain who to go to, because each person(s) offered something valuable. It was however, important to keep the focus on Tom, because he was the center for all of the discussions and if I could reach him, I would possibly be able to reach some of the other males in the room who felt the same way.

Lee Mun Wah's Intervention:

I asked Sarah how she felt about Tom, because I felt that he was not just defending the college, but also himself and that until he found that out, he would continually be in a defensive mode. Sarah told him that she didn't feel that way about him because she often felt he treated her fairly, but that his comment about "…rising to be a secretary" was insulting and sexist – and that surprised her.

I called on the other white male and he shared how he was upset with Tom's arrogance and ease in dismissing what Sarah had to say without asking her any questions or wanting to know more about her experiences. Tom listened intently to him and apologized to Sarah. I prompted him to ask her a question that would encourage her to say more.
I then asked the group if what happened was familiar to them.

Group/Dyad Process Questions:

1. What came up for you during this experience?

2. What was familiar? Why?

3. Why do you think Tom was defensive? Would you have been? Why?

4. Where do you think Tom got his notions about women "rising to be secretaries"?

5. Who did you identify with? Why?

6. What do you think was Tom's intent and what was the impact?

Summary:

1. Someone once said that just because we don't believe in something doesn't mean it doesn't exist. So that even though, as men, we never have to be afraid of our safety on a daily basis, that doesn't mean that women have the same experience. We need to open our eyes and to ask questions about the world around us. Especially from those whose lives and experiences are different from our own.

2. We are all recovering racists and sexists, the real question is what are we going to do about it? If not you, then who? If not now, then when?

3. If we are ever going to end racism or sexism, we need to be willing to look at ourselves and to take responsibility for our actions and our behaviors.

4. Though Tom's intent may have seemed good to him, the impact was very different than what he thought.

President of the Company

I was asked to present an Unlearning Racism Workshop to a company that I was told would not only be challenging, but also devoid of any emotions. The group was part of a mentorship program that had just started two years ago. All of the mentors were white males from the midwest and almost all the folks who were being mentored were men and women of color.

I started off with having the mentorees think about what it was like joining this company and how many of them thought they could be the President of the company someday. An Asian man, Ming Huan, raised his hand and formed it into a zero and yelled out, "Absolutely ZERO!" He then looked down angrily. All the white executives to his left turned their heads away from him, and the Asian woman, sitting next to Ming Huan, started weeping. There was an intense silence for almost 30 seconds, during which almost all the folks of color were just frowning, while most of the white managers turned red or stiffened – few looking at the Asian man.

Questions for the Facilitator:

1. What came up for you in reading this vignette?
2. What are some of the keywords that you should focus in on?
3. What do you think is going on for Ming Huan?
4. Why do you think the white managers looked away?
5. What's familiar about this vignette?
6. Who would you begin with?
7. What do you think that Ming wants? Why?
8. What do you think the managers are afraid of? Why?
9. What is hard about this vignette?

Lee Mun Wah's Thoughts:

I always knew I was impactful, but never to this degree or this quick in a workshop. This could either be construed as a wonderful opening or "Oh my god, what have I started here?" I chose to see it as an incredible opening, not just because Ming opened up, but because of the reactions of the executives and the persons of color. The veil had been lifted and the show was on! I was exhilarated and deeply moved at the same time. There have probably only been a handful of times I have witnessed the anguish of an Asian person, let alone a Chinese man, expressed so directly and physically. I was proud of him and at the same time deeply touched by what must have made him feel so desperate, so filled with hopelessness to say what he did and in the way that he did.

When the Asian woman next to him touched his hand and mourned with him, I knew that she understood what he had gone through, because it was probably her story, too. You could also see it in the faces and bodies of the persons of color throughout the room. What was also so very glaring was the stark contrast of the white folks in the room. They were obviously shocked. And yet, what was most telling was the way they responded – by looking away.

The question here was did the white folks notice that they had looked away and what did it mean? At the same time, I caught a glimpse of one white woman who started crying during Ming's outburst. What was her connection to him? She was also sitting with the people of color, while one of the other white women was wedged between two white men. Where everyone sat spoke volumes. Was this the clue that would unlock the secrets of this company's predominantly white culture? Would they be willing to tell the truth? Would Ming?

All of these people could lead to somewhere…

Whenever I am uncertain or overwhelmed by too many choices, I try to survey the room for someone of color and someone of EuroAmerican heritage. That way I balance the dialogue and thus enhance my possibilities. Also, this company needed to see people of color and whites in relationship – making mistakes, saying things that are misunderstood, crying or getting angry – and still staying in the room and facing each other.

Lee Mun Wah's Intervention:

I asked everyone what they noticed about the rest of the group when Ming Huan yelled out. Many shared how they noticed that the white managers all turned the opposite direction when Ming Huan got angry. I then asked the white managers what would be a good question to ask Ming Huan. One of them finally asked, "What came up for you when the question was asked about the President?" Ming Huan shared how hard it was to work here, never getting the sense that he was "executive" material because of his ethnicity.

Later on I opened the discussion up to the rest of the participants. The Asian woman shared that she felt so unappreciated for all of her hard work. She felt "invisible" in the eyes of the white supervisor. A white female manager shared that she had hired a lot of these new folks of color and that she felt that she had hired them under false pretenses because none of what she promised was really true. She had hoped the diversity initiatives they were working on would be in place during their tenure. Sadly, it didn't happen and almost 60% of those folks of color she recruited had left disillusioned and disappointed. A Latino man from that group shared how most of his colleagues had left, wondering why he was still there. He told his friends that he was thinking about leaving soon because he didn't have much of a chance here. He had dreamed of being a manager by now, which was part of his five-year plan, but now it was all but impossible. He came to realize that only white males had a chance here and that he and most of the people of color were just not what this company was looking for.

Group/Dyad Process Questions:

1. What came up for you about this experience?

2. What was familiar to you? Why?

3. Who did you identify with? Why?

4. What would you say to Ming Huan? Why?

5. If you had all the qualifications, do you think you could be the President? Why or why not?

Summary:

1. So often, we turn away when we don't know what to do or what to say. But, what today illustrates is that something doesn't go away just because we don't talk about it. Something painful doesn't go away just because we turn away from it. If we are willing to hear the truth and to ask questions, then we invite the possibilities for an authentic and heartfelt conversation about racism and other oppressive issues.

2. All I did today was ask a question: "How many of you believe you can be President of this company?" In less than five minutes, people shared something that they have never talked about in this company. The question is…do you want to know the truth, the whole truth?

3. Diversity is not a shiny brochure; it is in the faces and hearts of those people who work for you. They will encourage others to come to work here if they feel valued and acknowledged for who they are and what they can contribute.

No Child Left Behind

I was once asked to do a workshop in the Midwest because a Hmong child had just gotten beaten up by a group of skinheads. He was in the hospital with most of his front teeth knocked out by a bat. The community was shocked and wanted me to help them figure out how this could happen in their town and how they could talk about this peacefully.

Questions for the Facilitator:

1. What are your first impressions and feelings?
2. What scares you about doing this workshop?
3. What are your feelings about skinheads? Why?
4. What do you hope to offer these folks? Why?
5. Who would you work with first? Why?
6. What is your knowledge of the Hmong culture?
7. Why is it important for you and the community to know something about the Hmong culture?

Lee Mun Wah's Thoughts:

Looking at this experience through the lens of a person of color, I was able to sense the deeper issues that perhaps a person of privilege would miss. For example, one of the most common experiences of victims is that they feel isolated and alone during the incident – even though it may occur in a crowd of folks; usually no one steps forward or speaks in their defense.

Commonly, victims do not tell anyone because they might be questioned and interrogated as if they were the cause of the problem – that they had done something to provoke such a response. That was the suspicion voiced by some in this community.

In this case, the perpetrators looked like the majority in their community. Unless someone steps forward and shares their outrage or support, the family or victim will generalize about the whole community because of their silence and inaction.

There is another important point: When I hear some folks talk about how they wouldn't hurt anyone and that those who do are just ignorant, I feel that somehow the focus has now shifted to someone besides themselves. The perpetrators are always over there. There is not a sense of responsibility, self-reflection or need for action. So that even though they wouldn't act in such a racist manner, they seldom do anything on a daily basis to stop it or to help end it.

So, as you can see, a Mindful perspective means looking at a situation from the context of a person's life experiences – be it as a person of color, or as a EuroAmerican in the context of this dominant culture. They are all interrelated.

Lee Mun Wah's Intervention:

When I got there, I could see that the participants were scared and angry at the same time. I told the audience that in just a little while I would be leaving and that their answer to becoming a community again was right here in this room. I asked them what "community" meant for them. After a lot of discussion, I asked how many of them had gone to the hospital. As I looked out into the audience, I could see that they were afraid to look around, maybe out of fear that no one would raise their hand or that someone would notice that they hadn't.

Only one person answered. She said that the teacher of the child was the only one at the hospital from their community. I remembered being shocked, but then again, not really. I think that as a society, we have become detached from the violence around us. It is not until it happens to us or to someone we love that we begin to sense the impact of violence and racism on our communities.

After asking my question, I could see that the participants were visibly shaken. Many were crying and most just nodded their heads. Sometimes, as facilitators we forget to simply say the truth. We dance around the issue – when, in fact, the answer is right there in front of us. The truth always is.

I told the audience that if they did not go to the hospital, then this child's family would probably be leaving their city as soon as they could. And that until they embraced every child that is victimized as if they were their own, then they would never be truly a community in the very best sense of the word.

Group/Dyad Process Questions:

a.   What kind of environment encourages this kind of incident to happen?

b.   Where did those skinheads learn how to hate?

c.   How does this community deal with different cultures coming here to live?

d.   What have you taught your children about other cultures?

e.   When you heard what happened, what were your first reactions? Why?

f.   Are there racist attitudes and behaviors in this community? If so, how are you a part of the solution/problem?

g.   What do you think it will take for this Hmong family and their son to want to stay here? Do you want them to stay/leave?

Summary:

1.   As I said when I came in, the real work of keeping this community safe will be the responsibility of each person here. To have this young boy's family stay here will only happen if they feel you are willing to rid this community of the environment that fosters this kind of hatred and fear.

2.   It is easy to blame some group or individual for the hatred that led to this violent act, but that would be too easy. Someone once asked me how to end racism and I said, "That's easy. Begin with the person next to you and with yourself."

Our company has a motto: "If not you, then who? If not now, then when?"

Racists Are Just Ignorant

An older Japanese man, Yoshi, who was very muscular, stood up and shared how when he was growing up his family couldn't buy a house in a white neighborhood and how hard it was during the war against Japan. He also talked about how his two daughters, who went to college last year, experienced racist remarks from students and other instructors. When I asked him how he felt about his children's experiences on the campus, he quickly belted out, "I just tell my girls – they're just ignorant folks! Just get your grades and we'll show them with our big homes and our high paying jobs." Everyone laughed and he got a standing ovation and quickly sat down.

Questions for the Facilitator:

1. What came up for you in reading this vignette?
2. What are the keywords to focus in on?
3. What are some of Yoshi's issues?
4. What is your reaction to the group? Why?
5. What is hard about this vignette?
6. Who would you work with first? Why?
7. What does Yoshi need?
8. What is familiar about Yoshi's attitude and behavior?
9. How would you incorporate the group into your intervention?
10. What is Yoshi not saying?

Lee Mun Wah's Thoughts:

Yoshi struck me as a very confident and proud Japanese man. He had learned how to get an applause from his white counterparts by simply telling them that nothing could hurt him or his daughters. His daughters were going to be successful, educationally and financially, no matter what was done to them. The enemy was over there and they were over here. This type of appeasement and assimilation is so familiar to me. And yet, each time I am amazed at how unconscious white folks are in perpetuating this type of exchange. The advantage of this type of exchange is that it gets white folks off the hook from having to take any action or to reflect on their own participation and responsibility in promoting racism. Everyone leaves safely and cleanly. Don't ask, don't tell.

So the real work here was to find a way to have Yoshi share what he was really feeling and at the same time, to open the eyes of the white folks to their colluding with Yoshi to stay silent. I also wanted to get to Yoshi's life as a Japanese boy and eventually in the armed forces. Both would shed some light on his emotional and professional development and assimilation. Perhaps I needed to find an opening that would connect Yoshi and myself. Upon reflection, we had more in common than I thought.

Lee Mun Wah's Intervention:

I touched Yoshi's shoulder with my hand and told him that as a father myself, I wondered how it must have been to work so hard to make sure his daughters were going to have a better world than he did, then to find out that no matter how smart, how responsible or how nice they were – they still were victims of racism. He broke down and cried and talked about how hard it was to realize that the racism he faced as a child was still alive and well for his daughters. I then asked him what it was like here at this agency, as a Japanese man, and he looked at me with opened eyes and shook his head, "You have no idea what it has been like all these years. You just come to accept it and hope that it just goes away, but it never does. You just try to not let it get you down. But it hasn't been easy."

Group/Dyad Process Questions:

1. What came up for you listening to Yoshi?

2. Why do you think Yoshi kept his silence?

3. What's familiar to you about Yoshi's experience?

4. How many of you are parents? How many of you have had to tell your children that no matter what they achieve or who they become professionally, at any given moment, they can become a victim of racism?

5. At what age did you experience racism? What was it like for you?

6. What did you learn about today? How did it move you?

7. How many of you were told by your parents about the racism you might face? What was it like for you being told? How did it affect you?

Summary:

1. As you can see from today, one of the hardest things to endure as a person of color is having to live with the reality that you cannot protect your children from racism. And for those of you who h-ave never had to tell your children – how lucky you are. I hated telling my son at the age of six what he would be facing because he was Guatemalan. I had to tell him because he had already experienced racism at the age of three.

2. I want you to hear what it has taken for Yoshi to get to this room. What he has had to endure. The question is…do you want to know? Do you want to do something about it?

Martin Luther King Jr. was right, *"Real peace is not the absence of conflict. It has always been the presence of justice."*

Why Didn't He Tell Me?

A woman from California named Michelle, of Japanese and Irish heritage, shared how she went to a family reunion in Louisiana with her Dad. She was devastated because no one would talk with her. Some of the relatives even made Jap jokes in front of her and everyone laughed. She ran out of their home crying and extremely angry. She said she was upset that her Irish father had not told her what she might be facing when she came with him, but even angrier at herself for not being able to say something back when they made their ethnic slurs about Japanese.

Questions for the Facilitator:

1. What came up for you?
2. What are some of the keywords?
3. Who is Michelle angry with? Why?
4. Why do you think her Dad didn't tell her about her relatives?
5. What is Michelle asking for? Why?
6. Who would you work with first? Why?
7. How would you like this to turn out? Why?
8. What is hard about this situation?
9. How would you include the group?

Lee Mun Wah's Thoughts:

Working with Michelle was not going to be easy. She was very shy telling her story and kept looking away or down. I sensed from her body language that she had difficulty with anger, possibly because of her being Japanese and possibly from other family experiences dealing with conflict. She expressed being angry at herself for not being able to communicate her hurt and anguish at her relatives. I sensed some shame and a sense of betrayal.

My first instincts told me that bringing her back to the scene of the crime would help her. She needed to go back to complete what was unfinished – an acknowledgement that her feelings of racism and betrayal were justified. She also needed an apology that was heartfelt and personal from her relatives and especially from her father. From a larger perspective, she also needed a sense of community to support her as she moved on into a new awareness of having a larger family identity, and with that, the struggles of being multi-ethnic.

Lee Mun Wah's Intervention:

Michelle had difficulty talking about how angry she felt, so I had her pick out members of the audience to role play her family in Louisiana and her father. Through several practices, she was finally able to tell her relatives how angry she was at their jokes and how hurt she was with her father for not warning her or protecting her.

I also had Michelle tell her relatives what she had hoped they would have been like. Michelle shared that she wanted to be greeted warmly and embraced as part of the family. Each member of the role play embraced and welcomed her into the family. She cried and said that this was what she had always wanted – to have both sides of her acknowledged and celebrated.

I then asked the Asians and the EuroAmericans in the room to hold hands and to form a circle around her. Those of mixed heritage said that this, too, had always been their dream – to not have to choose, but to have all sides of themselves celebrated and joined together.

Group/Dyad Process Questions:

1. Who did you identify with? Why?

2. Why do you think Michelle had a hard time connecting with her anger?

3. What would you have done if you were Michelle? Why?

4. What was familiar about Michelle's experience for you?

5. If you were her father, what would you have done? Why?

6. What did you learn from this experience?

Summary:

1. Multi-ethnic children are the largest growing group in the United States. They will be facing prejudice from those who feel they are not ethnic enough or too white. We must talk about what they are experiencing and take a look at how we define who a multi-ethnic person is. These children are the pioneers of a new culture – multi-cultural – and they will need our support and acceptance.

2. Folks like Michelle must hear that it is not they who are out of place, but rather our insecurities and our fears about difference that separate us.

3. We are rapidly becoming another generation that seldom hears an apology or is held accountable for one's actions or attitudes. We must begin modeling for our children the gift of saying we are sorry and looking at how we are a part of the problem and the solution.

This Workshop Is Police Bashing!

A black male, Thomas, shared in the workshop how he was beaten and thrown up against a police car while being questioned for no apparent reason. I asked the audience to raise their hands if this story was familiar to them. Most of the people of color raised their hands. As some of them were sharing their stories, a white woman, Susan, jumped up and yelled, "This workshop is police bashing!"

Questions for the Facilitator:

1. What came up for you about this vignette?
2. What are some of the keywords to focus in on?
3. What are the issues sitting in the middle of the room?
4. What do you think are Susan's issues with the workshop? Why?
5. What's familiar about this situation?
6. What do you think Susan wants? Why?
7. Why do you think Susan is so angry?
8. Who would you work with first?
9. How would you include the group?

Lee Mun Wah's Thoughts:

I wasn't surprised by Susan's remark, but rather by her intensity and passion. I had a feeling that there was something very personal about her reaction. She just wasn't someone who didn't believe their stories, but rather someone who had a deeper stake in these stories.

Once again, there was a story behind Susan's statement. It was what she wasn't saying that needed to be shared, and from there, a larger dialogue between the victims and their perpetrators and the larger community. Those who told their stories had created an opening for everyone else.

What was also important here was not to forget the trauma of the victims who shared their stories of racism and police harassment – they too, needed to be acknowledged and supported, and for some action to be taken. And in the process, to discover how many in the audience didn't believe the victims either, or felt it was police bashing, too.

Lee Mun Wah's Intervention:

I told Susan that I had a hunch that I wanted to check out. "Do you have a partner or a relative in law enforcement?" She said, "Yes", and started to cry out loud. I then asked her what that was like and she poured her heart out about how hard it was to see him go out at night, not knowing if he'd come back. She apologized for being so outspoken, but wanted people to know that her husband really cared about people, too.

Group/Dyad Process Questions:

1. What came up for you during this experience?

2. Who did you identify with? Why?

3. What was good about this and what was hard? Why?

4. What do Thomas and Susan have in common?

5. What came up for you when most of the people of color raised their hands?

6. What would be a good question to ask them?

Summary:

1. So you see, if I hadn't asked what was underneath Susan's remark, we would never have known the deeper story behind her words. Everyone has a story, and if we don't jump too quickly into being defensive or adversarial, we can learn about their lives and what they have gone through to get to this room today.

2. There are good law enforcement officers everywhere and their jobs are important and perilous at the same time. But, like all professions, there are also ones that use their positions to harm others, who act out racism and sexism, and it is imperative to bring them to justice. The harm that they do not only robs individuals of their dignity and well being, but also tarnishes a community's reputation and sense of safety for all its citizens.

3. Susan, I heard you say that your husband cares for justice. In that case, I have a hunch that he would not stand for the things that happened to these folks. When he and members of this community stand together and say no more, then it will exemplify the very best in a community – ensuring happiness and equal protection for all its citizens. Would your husband be willing to meet these folks and see what he can do to help? She was certain that he would be willing to. The audience applauded.

Diversity Exercises

To see the preciousness of all things,
we must bring our full attention to life.

\~Jack Kornfield

Insider/Outsider Exercise

The goal of this exercise is to exemplify the effect of exclusion and inclusion on our self-esteem and personal choices, as well as to identify the techniques we create to survive and to assimilate.

Time Needed: This exercise takes about 45-60 minutes.

Instructions:

I need ten volunteers to form two groups. You will be called Insiders.
Now I need two volunteers to meet me outside of the room. You will be called Outsiders.

Insiders Instructions: (Those in the room)

Form two groups that are gender and ethnically balanced.

When the two folks come in, try to keep them out, short of any violence or physical force.

Outsiders Instructions: (Those outside the room)

When you come in try to be a part of any of the groups, short of any violence or physical force.

Audience:

You will be observing the process. Please note how decisions are made and who makes them. Pay close attention to the reactions of the participants. Please do not laugh or talk during the process so that the folks stay in role play mode.

Time:

Allot up to 5 minutes for the Outsiders to try and get into the groups.
Keep note when the Outsiders give up, when and why. Notice the process of exclusion.

Debriefing Process Questions:

Insiders:

What kinds of feelings came up for you?
What kinds of strategies did your group use?
What was hard about this exercise?
What was familiar about this exercise for you?
If you didn't want to keep anyone out, what made you do it?
What would've been the consequences if you chose not to keep anyone out?
What were your opinions of the Outsiders? Did they try hard enough? What could they have done differently?

Outsiders:

What was it like for you to be an Outsider?
What kinds of strategies did you use to get in?
What was familiar about this exercise?
How long do you think this exercise lasted?
As you were being excluded, did you ever think that it was because of your ethnicity or gender?
What do you think are the consequences to an agency/company when folks are excluded?

Audience:

What did you observe?
What was familiar? Does this happen here?
Who were the leaders? Who were the silent ones?
Who were the weak links? Why?
What do you think are the consequences to your agency/company when an individual or group is excluded?

Facilitator's Summary:

Notice how each Insider was only able to do this exercise if they didn't look at the Outsider's eyes. Often we can justify what we do if we objectify or label those we exclude, using words like aliens, foreigners, immigrants, gooks.

Notice that though the Insiders didn't want to exclude the Outsiders, they did so because of team pressure or working towards a common goal. At some given moment in our lives, we each have been excluded.

Notice the amount of energy and strategies that the Outsiders had to use to get in.

Imagine what that might be like every day and for years to come. If you don't have to plan a strategy to survive, why not? How are you different or the same as some of the Outsiders or Insiders here today?

What does a company lose when folks are excluded? What does an agency/company gain when folks feel appreciated and valued?

We often blame the Outsider for creating their predicament. For example: They should have done it this way, they didn't try hard enough, they weren't smart enough, they were too uneducated, they were too loud, too silent, too vocal, too impatient. Sound familiar?

What are some of the obstacles that keep folks excluded? For example: They need to get more experience, more degrees, more communications skills, social skills, different clothing (or to look more professional), less of an accent (unless you are French or English). And if you achieve all of the above, we might just have an opening in five years. Anyone interested?

What were you like on the first day you came here and what are you like now? What happened or didn't happen?

Invisibility Exercise

This is one of my favorite exercises because it is so simple, yet effective. It illustrates the pervasiveness of racism and sexism in our daily lives. I often use this exercise with audiences/agencies that believe that they are free of racism or have nothing else to learn about racist or sexist issues.

Time Needed: 15 minutes

Instructions:

The exercise begins with the facilitator walking out into the audience and shaking hands with someone who looks like him/her. It is more effective if it is a person of color.

Facilitator: Hello. What is your name? Welcome.

(Turning to the audience): Raise your hand if you noticed what I did.
(Do not call on any women or people of color).

Facilitator only calls on four white men, one at a time, who haven't raised their hands, and asks them, "What did you notice that I did just now?"

(The idea of this exercise is to show how quickly people of color and women will eventually stop raising their hands in anticipation of not being called on).

Debriefing Questions:

1. How many of you noticed what happened?

2. How many of you noticed that I didn't call on any women or people of color? How did that make you feel? If you didn't notice, why not?

3. How many of you noticed that I only called on white males who didn't raise their hands? If you didn't notice, why not?

4. I did this to show you that in less than one minute, I could get the women and the people of color to stop raising their hands. Why do you think they stopped raising their hands? You see, that is what racism and sexism is all about – the devaluation of people based on their gender, race, age, or sexual orientation. After awhile they stop participating and contributing and we wonder why they are just followers or, perhaps, so passive. The reason I said hello to this particular person was because so many times I am the only one who looks (facilitator's ethnicity) in a room. So, I am always on the lookout for someone who looks like me. How many of you know exactly what I am talking about?

Note: this exercise works best for facilitators of color.

Racial Assessment Exercise

The Racial Assessment is therapeutically used to help individual participants share the trauma of racism on their lives without having to tell their personal stories unless they choose to. This particular exercise brings the issue of racism into the room and into the workplace. It personalizes the victim's history and experiences. Therapeutically, it allows the victims to release their anguish and hurt, as well as the opportunity to receive acknowledgement, validation and support. The possibility for healing is one of the paramount goals of this exercise, because it is a stimulus for institutional commitment and change.

Time Needed: Up to one hour

Instructions:

Facilitator: The most important question for a multicultural nation is the least asked question in any corporation, government agency, or educational institution, "What has your life been like getting from there to here in terms of your racial history or racial experiences. Because it can profoundly explain why you relate or don't relate to certain ethnicities."

So, we are going to take a Racial Assessment of every person in this room, and we are going to do this without your having to say a single word.

Now breathe…

What I am going to do is ask a question and if it pertains to you, please stand up without saying a word. Also, please don't laugh during this exercise, because if you have ever been a victim of racism, it is neither funny nor something you ever forget.

Please stand …(in between each statement, ask the audience to look around and see who is standing and who is sitting):

1. If when you turn on the television or open up the newspaper, you will see people of your race widely represented.

2. If when you use a check or credit card, the color of your skin will not be used against you.

3. If when you do well in a challenging situation, you will not be told that you are a credit to your race. (The assumption is that you are an exception to others of your race).

4. If when interviewing for a job, you can reasonably be assured that the interviewer will be a member of your racial group.

5. If the head of your company or agency is a member of your racial group.

6. If when you decide to rent or purchase housing, you can reasonably be assured that because of your color, your neighbors will be neutral or pleasant to you and your family.

7. If you can buy posters, postcards, picture books, greeting cards, dolls, toys, and children's magazines featuring people of your race.

8. If, when shopping, you can reasonably be assured that if you are followed or harassed by the store management or security guard, it is not because of the color of your skin.

9. If, when shopping, you have been followed by the store management or security guard because of the color of your skin.

10. If you have changed your name or had it changed for you, because people couldn't pronounce it.

11. If you have ever been told or heard from others that you and your people don't belong here and should leave.

12. If the police have ever stopped you in your car or on the street because of your ethnic or racial heritage.

13. If you have ever thought of not having any children or any more children because of racism.

Optional: At any point in these statements, while the participants are standing, you can ask any individual what it was like for them to be treated like this. Refer to Mindful Inquiry for additional questions to ask.

**Inspired by Peggy McIntosh

The State of Diversity Exercise

The theory behind this exercise is to illustrate the reality of diversity in most companies/ agencies in this country, as well as what is needed in the workplace for a truly multicultural environment.

Time Needed: 5 minutes

Instructions:

If you would like to know the state of diversity at your company, please raise your hand. Wonderful. So, what we are going to do right now is take a cultural assessment that won't require any writing or speaking, and most of all, any money. In fact, you can do it right where you are sitting. Everyone, please stand.

Imagine that you are one of five candidates chosen to be the next President of this company. You have all the skills and experience that are needed.

Please sit down if you think….

1. That your gender will be issue.

2. That your age will be an issue.

3. That your ethnic or racial heritage will be an issue.

4. That your religious affiliation will be an issue.

5. That your sexual orientation will be an issue.

6. That your physical disability will be an issue.

7. That your accent will be an issue.

8. That the job will probably be given to someone who knows someone in the company.

9. Notice who is standing and who is not.

Facilitator's Group Process Questions:

Ladies and gentlemen, notice how many were standing before we began and how many are now left. What do you see?

Imagine what a company loses and what it can gain if people believe that if they had the skills and experience, they could become the President of your company. Imagine what they would bring to your company.

If you really want to know what the state of diversity of your company is, just ask folks, "What were you like when you first came here and what are you like now?"

Business Case For Hiring

This exercise illustrates the disparity between those who have power and those who don't – those who make decisions and those who merely implement decisions.

Time Needed: 10 minutes

Instructions: To the audience:

1. What is the business case for hiring *women?*

2. What is the business case for hiring *people of color?*

3. What is the business case for hiring *gays & lesbians?*

4. What is the business case for hiring folks with *physical disabilities?*

5. What is the business case for hiring folks who are *younger? Older?*

6. What is the business case for hiring folks who are *immigrant born?*

Facilitator's Process Questions (to the audience):

1. How did it feel to have to rationalize why you should be here?

2. Who is missing? Why?

3. Who gets to ask these questions?

4. Who gets to decide what is the best business case and who belongs?

5. Who gets to make up these questions?

6. How did white men inherit this powerful position?

7. How and when did these types of questions come into being?

Orange Toss Exercise

The purpose of this exercise is to illustrate how the impact of gender and race and other diversity issues affect our roles in relationships and workplace dynamics.

Time Needed: 45–60 minutes

Instructions:

1. Form groups of 4-10 (depending on the size of your entire group).
2. Pass out four oranges to each group.
3. Each person in the group must touch each orange no more than once. Strategize how you would like that to happen.
4. Now we are going to time how long it takes for everyone in your group to touch the orange once.
5. Now we would like you to find a way that best works for your group to touch each orange once. You have two more tries.
6. Thank you everyone. Now let's evaluate what just occurred.

Note: You can process with them in their small groups or all together.

Debriefing Process Questions:

1. What was it like for you doing this exercise?

2. What kind of role did you play in this group? The same or different in life?

3. Who were the leaders and who were the followers?

4. Did you feel listened to or ignored? Why or why not?

5. Did you feel like a team, or were there distinct person(s) who made most of the decisions?

6. How did gender affect how decisions were made or not made?

7. In the future would you have done anything differently?

8. Did you notice who was ignored and who was paid attention to?

9. Did you speak up when others were mistreated? Why or why not?

10. What kinds of non-verbal messages did you observe?

11. Who were the ones who wanted to play by the rules and which ones wanted to be more spontaneous? Which were you?

12. How is this game like your workplace environment and dynamics?

Conflict History Assessment

This exercise is designed to show the impact of one's life experiences with conflict on present day behavior and attitudes.

Time Needed: 60-90 minutes

Instructions:

Break up into groups of 4-6 participants. One of you will be the Observer, Speaker or Listener. All of you will rotate being Observer, Listener or Speaker.

Observer: Keeps time and gives one minute warning.

Speaker: (5 minutes) Answers questions below.

Listener: (up to 5 minutes) Reflects back to Speaker what was shared.

Speaker: (3 minutes) Gives feedback to Listener on effectiveness.

Observer: (3 minutes) Shares observations about the whole process.

Group Process: (up to 10 minutes) Processes any feelings/responses.

Questions for Speaker:

1. How was *conflict* dealt with in your family?

2. How did it *affect* you when it happened?

3. How does it *affect* you today? In your relationships and at work?

4. How do you *compensate* for it so that nobody knows?

5. What do you *need* to feel supported around this issue?

Differences Exercise

The theory behind this exercise is to illustrate our fears of identifying racial differences because of negative connotations related to our learned stereotypes of each other. This exercise is a good supplement to the Racial Assessment Exercise.

Time Needed: 10 to 20 minutes.

Instructions:

Choose two folks who are ethnically different (preferably one is an African American male of muscular build). Do not let the audience know that is the reason you chose them.

Facilitator: What are your names?

(To Audience): In what ways are these two different from each other?

Take up to 15 observations from the audience. Wait until someone mentions their ethnicities. If not, begin the following:

1. I would like you to notice that nobody mentioned their ethnicities.

2. Often we avoid saying our own or someone else's ethnicities.

3. The way we avoid pointing out differences is by saying:

> We're just human beings.
> I don't see color.
> I'm colorblind.

4. I think we avoid looking at or identifying color because we see differences as having a negative connotation.

5. Let me show you what I mean. Imagine that (the African American man) is attending college. This is what he might hear or witness when he gets there (whisper into the ear of different folks in the audience):

> I wonder what sport he's in?
> He doesn't look very smart.
> I bet he does poorly in science and math.

Or maybe when he goes onto corporate America, this is what he might hear or witness (whisper into the ear of different folks in the audience):

I didn't know we had an affirmative action program here.
Why is he here? We already have two blacks.
I heard he has a doctorate. I bet it's from a small college.
He doesn't look very smart or responsible. I wonder how he got in?
I don't think he has much experience. He's got to prove it to me.
I heard he knew someone in the company.
He looks pretty volatile.
I'm afraid he might have a bad temper or can get out of control.
We need to keep an eye on him. He looks like the lazy type.
He seems kind of uppity to me for a black man.

(Turning to African American man): Now, I don't know you. I just met you today. Have you ever had any of these experiences? Do any of these sound familiar to you? Which ones?

How many of you know_____? (the African American man)

How many of you knew these things happened to him?

The question is not just why don't you know, but why didn't he tell you?

(To the African American man) Would you be willing to tell them how you felt when these things happened to you? How have those things affected you today? In your relationships? At work?

(To the audience) What did you notice as he was sharing his life?

Yes, it was like it happened yesterday. The pain of it is still with him.

Let's give him a big hand.

In just a short time we learned about his life in ways that we may never have gotten to know if we didn't ask. It's time to stop our "I won't ask and you won't tell" policy in this country.

To end racism in this country, we need to learn about the people around us. We need to be willing to hear the truth and to act on what we hear.

Emotions Exercise

The objective of this exercise is to show the effect that our past experiences have on our present day behavior. If we don't ask questions about the context of one's life, we are prone to stereotyping and not knowing who they truly are and why.

Time Needed: Up to 45 minutes.

Instructions:

1. Have each participant write on their name tags an emotion that they fear.

2. In dyads, share with your partner the following questions:

a. What emotion are you afraid of?

b. Where did your fear come from (family, friends, school)?

c. How did it affect you growing up?

d. How does it affect you today? In your workplace, relationships?

e. How do you compensate for it (how do you keep others from knowing)?

Ancestral Exercise

Have everyone break up into dyads. One will listen for five minutes and the other will speak. At the end of five minutes they will switch. The Listener is not to say anything, just be attentive. Please avoid laughing or asking any questions. The Speaker shall answer these questions:

1. What is your name? What is your *real* name? (Many have had their names changed because of racism).

2. What is your ethnicity?

3. What is good about being (your ethnic group)?

4. What is hard about being (your ethnic group)?

**Have the group process their feelings and interactions.

Withholding Exercise

The purpose of this exercise is to allow space for any individual(s) who have withheld something from someone, either positive or negative, for whatever reasons, and would like to share how they feel with that person or group. This is a good way to model dealing with conflict as a part of relationships, rather than only reacting when there is a crisis.

Time Needed: Up to 60 minutes (depending on number of issues and group dynamics)

Instructions:

Facilitator: There is a saying, "If not you, then who? If not now, then when?"

We are now going to open the group up for anyone who has a withhold about someone. A withhold is something that has happened that affects how we feel about someone, which can either be positive or negative, but keeps us apart.

We encourage you to use this time well so that you don't leave here feeling unfinished or incomplete.

Guidelines to Withholds:

1. If someone raises his/her hand, ask him/her to share her/his name and the person they have a withhold about.

2. Next, ask permission of the person that is identified, "Would you be open to working this out?" Most will say yes; if not, ask why?

3. Use Conflict Facilitation Model and Mindful Inquiry to help with your mediation.

*Note: This exercise requires advanced facilitation skills and/or conflict mediation training.

Alliance Group Exercise

This exercise allows the participants to plan for their next steps to promote diversity, while at the same time acknowledging their fears and their need for support.

Time Needed: Up to 25 minutes

Instructions: Form groups of 4-6 and answer the following questions:

1. What are you willing to do *personally* to promote diversity in your relationships, in your agency, in your community?

2. What are some of the *obstacles* you may encounter?

3. What do you *need* to be successful in your endeavor?

4. What do you need to feel *supported* in your endeavor?

5. *Who* do you need that support from? Why?

Learning the Truth Exercise

This exercise is about revealing the truth about what it is like in our workplaces when someone is not valued or acknowledged or supported.

Time Needed: Up to 15 minutes.

Instructions:

Pair up with someone who you don't know and who is different than you.

One of you will listen and one of you will speak for five minutes, and then you will switch.

The listener will ask:

"What is it like for you as a (gender and ethnic group) here at this agency/company?"

"How do you feel supported or unsupported to be successful?"

Ready, begin.

Debriefing Questions:

Process as a whole group. As each person shares, ask the group:

"Who knows exactly what this person is talking about? What's familiar?"

Optional Questions:

1. What has this company/agency lost when you can't be yourself?

2. How are you different from when you first started and how you are now?

3. What do you need in order for you to feel successful here?

4. If you were the President of this company, what would you change?

 StirFry Seminars

Private Seminars & Trainings

StirFry Seminars & Consulting

Since its founding in 1994, StirFry Seminars & Consulting has revolutionized the field of diversity through its internationally acclaimed documentary films and seminars. Millions of viewers worldwide have seen The Color of Fear, as well as many of the other groundbreaking films produced and directed by Lee Mun Wah, StirFry's founder, CEO and Master Trainer. In 1995, Oprah Winfrey produced a one-hour special on Lee Mun Wah's life and the impact of *The Color of Fear*.

Thousands of participants from educational, government, corporate and social service agencies have taken StirFry's trainings and seminars so that they could then begin facilitating discussion groups in their agencies, schools, and communities and learn to engage in authentic and healthy multicultural dialogue. The company is recognized by many of the top 500 corporations as having one of the most outstanding cross-cultural and communications training programs for managers, supervisors, H.R. and top administrative executives. Clients have relayed that their participation in our workshops has been life changing, powerful and applicable to their personal and professional lives.

StirFry Seminars & Consulting is represented by a multicultural staff of trainers and facilitators from a variety of professional backgrounds and diversity expertise. They each have years of experience working with corporations, government agencies, educational institutions and various social agencies.

Lee Mun Wah, Director

StirFry Seminars & Trainings

PRIVATE SEMINARS FOR CORPORATIONS:

Seminars
Unlearning Racism in the Workplace
A Cross Gender Conversation in the Workplace
Film Series Program (4-7 Hour Programs)
Unlearning Homophobia & Heterosexism in the Workplace
Diversity Conversations in the Workplace
How to Manage Diversity Conflicts & Communication Issues
A Dialogue on Gay & Lesbian Issues in the Workplace
Fireside Conversations about Diversity Issues
The Color of Fear - 3 Day Retreat
Introduction to Alliance Building in the Workplace (Parts One & Two)
A Cross Cultural Conversation – 3 Day Retreat
Preparing for a Global Market

Trainings
Ten Part Communications Training Program
Five Part Diversity Communications Program
Mindfully Resolving Conflicts
Film Facilitation Trainings Program
Cross Gender Conversations Training Program
Diversity Mediation Training Program

Organizational Development
Managing Organizational Conflict
Participating in a Changing Workforce
Embracing Team Membership within the Company Vision
Manager as Coach – Creating the Coaching Environment
Manager as Coach- Coaching Through Conflict
Manager as Coach – Reading Between the Lines
Professional Diversity Management
Visionary Leadership
Team Rhythm

Keynotes:
Walking Across the Room
An Unfinished Conversation
The World Is All Around Us
Conflict in the Workplace
A Promise Still to Keep
What Stands Between Us
Only a World Away
The Art of Mindfully Being Present

PRIVATE SEMINARS FOR EDUCATORS, STUDENTS, ADMINISTRATORS & STAFF:

Seminars
Unlearning Racism in the Classroom
A Cross Gender Conversation
Diversity Conversations in the Classroom
If These Halls Could Talk
Resolving Diversity Conflicts in the Classroom
Creating Community in a Diverse School Environment
A Conversation on Homophobia & Heterosexism

Trainings
Creating Community & Understanding Across Cultures
Diversity Mediation Training
Ten Part Communications Program
Five Part Diversity Communications Program
Mindfully Resolving Conflicts Training Program
Film Facilitation Trainings Program
Cross Gender Conversations Training Program

Keynotes
Walking Across the Classroom
An Unfinished Conversation
The World Is All Around Us
Conflict in Our Halls
A Promise Still to Keep
What Stands Between Us
Only a World Away
Creating Bridges in Our Schools
What's Missing in Our Classrooms?
If These Halls Could Talk

PRIVATE SEMINARS FOR SOCIAL SERVICE PROVIDERS:

Seminars
A Dialogue on Racism
A Cross Gender Conversation
The Practice of Honoring Diversity
Mindfully Resolving Cross Cultural Conflicts
Creating Community in Small Diverse Group Settings
A Conversation on Homophobia & Heterosexism
The Color of Fear - 3 Day Retreat
Alliance Building Across Cultures

Trainings
Mindfully Resolving Conflicts Training Program
Ten Part Communications Program
Five Part Diversity Communications Program
Using Films on Diversity to Create Cross Cultural Dialogues
Cross Gender Conversations Training
Working with Diverse Groups

Keynotes
Walking Across the Room
An Unfinished Conversation
The World Is All Around Us
Conflict in Our Workplaces
A Promise Still to Keep
What Stands Between Us
Only a World Away

PRIVATE SEMINARS FOR GOVERNMENT AGENCIES:

Seminars
Unlearning Racism in the Workplace
A Cross Gender Conversation in the Workplace
Film Series Program (4-7 Hour Programs)
Unlearning Homophobia & Heterosexism in the Workplace
Diversity Conversations in the Workplace
How to Manage Diversity Conflicts & Communication Issues
A Dialogue On Gay & Lesbian Issues in the Workplace
Fireside Conversations about Diversity Issues
The Color of Fear - 3 Day Retreat
Introduction to Alliance Building in the Workplace (Part One)
Multicultural Alliances in the Workplace (Part Two)
A Cross Cultural Conversation – 3 Day Retreat
Thinking Globally/Acting Locally on Diversity Issues
How to Facilitate & Stimulate Diversity Conversations Across Cultures

Trainings
Ten Part Communications Program
Five Part Diversity Communications Program
Mindfully Resolving Conflicts Training Program
Film Facilitation Trainings Program
Cross Gender Conversations Training Program
Diversity Mediation Training

Keynotes:
Walking Across the Room
An Unfinished Conversation
The World Is All Around Us
Conflict in the Workplace
A Promise Still to Keep
What Stands Between Us
Only a World Away
The Art of Mindfully Being Present
The Global Market Next Door

Berkeley, California Diversity Trainings for Individuals

We offer on-going diversity coursework at our Quan Yin Training Center for Compassionate Change in Berkeley, California. Most of these courses are held in a weekend format (Friday/Saturday/Sunday) but we also offer summer intensives. The fee for attending each course is dependent upon your organizational affiliation and is on a sliding scale. Go to http://www.stirfryseminars.com/BTC for more information and to print out the pdf registration forms to register by mail or fax.

Examples of courses that we have offered include:

- *Unlearning Racism, Sexism and Heterosexism Seminars*
- *Mastering Diversity Training & Facilitation*
- *Cross-Cultural Facilitation Skills for Diversity Trainers, Educators and Therapists*
- *Film Facilitation Training*
- *Cultural Competency for Leaders*

Some Background

Since 1971, Lee Mun Wah has been developing his skills as a facilitator, community therapist, filmmaker, educator, and diversity trainer. Early on, he realized that traditional methods of facilitation, group process and therapy did not adequately address such issues as racism, sexism and cross-cultural communications and conflicts. Over a span of 20 years, he developed a technique called *The Art of Mindful Facilitation* - a unique way of relating and observing from an Asian and Buddhist perspective. In 2004 he wrote, *The Art of Mindful Facilitation* and a training supplement, *The Art of Mindful Facilitation Training Film* outlining his theories and practices.

One of the areas that he focused on was the theory of intent & impact. Lee Mun Wah noticed that the western culture paid very little attention to the issue of *intent* and *impact* when communicating. Lee Mun Wah felt that by observing the impact of our communications, we could discover whether or not our communications were effective or ineffective. If they were ineffective, we could explore what occurred, inquire about our intent and impact, as well as reflecting on what transpired for each person - from a historical, emotional, social and physical perspective.

Another important area of focus was listening for the "key words" within our communications that could identify our needs and concerns. Lee Mun Wah long felt that part of the dissonance in our communications was due to our need to "solve" a situation, rather than to truly hear what was needed and felt. For Lee Mun Wah, simply sharing that one understood or heard someone was not enough. He felt that it was essential to inquire, "What did you understand? What did you hear?" From there, a bridge of understanding and trust could be built upon through continuous inquiry and personal disclosures.

DIVERSITY TRAINING FILMS (dvd format)

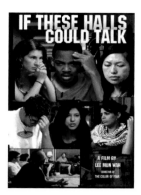

If These Halls Could Talk explores the myriad ways educators can learn how to develop authentic classroom environments where diversity issues can be discussed openly and safely. Through stories and personal exchanges, eleven students from various colleges and personal backgrounds share what makes it unsafe for them in the classroom and what it is like to be a minority/immigrant on a predominantly white campus. They explore issues of trust and distrust amongst one another, with other students and college staff/faculty. Lee Mun Wah models, for the first time, how to facilitate interpersonal conflicts and diversity issues mindfully and transformatively in the classroom. (2014)

If These Halls Could Talk is a package DVD set that includes:

Disc 1: "The Director's Cut" (97 min)
Disc 2: "The Director's Cut: Film Vignettes & Guide" (95 min) **and**, the "Classroom Edition: Film Vignettes & Guide" (2 hrs/45 min)

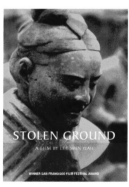

Stolen Ground is an award-winning film about six Asian men who spend a weekend together in Berkeley, California dispelling the myth of the "model minority." They share the struggles that Asians experience because of racism and the stereotypes that inhibit and diminish the importance of their heritage and cultural contributions. (1993 - 43 mins.)

Attention: Individuals and Students!

Now Announcing

On Demand Digital Streaming Rentals!

www.diversitytrainingfilms.com
Get access to StirFry films from the comfort of your home for a small fee; rentals provide online access for 24-hours.

The Color of Fear 1 is an internationally acclaimed film about eight men of various ethnicities engaging in an intimate and honest dialogue about race and the effects of racism on their lives and families. In 1995 Oprah Winfrey aired a one-hour special on Lee Mun Wah and The Color of Fear cast, which was viewed by over 15 million people around the world. (1994 - 90 mins.)

The Color of Fear 2: Walking Each Other Home reveals the unique and intimate relationship that eight men developed as they shared their experiences with racism. It shows what happened when the men came to an impasse during their weekend together, as well as who emerged to break the silence between them. (1995 - 56 mins.)

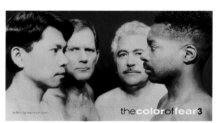

The Color of Fear 3 is an intimate conversation on what it means to be gay in this society and the impact it has on one's sense of safety and identity. Through personal stories and interactions, we have a glimpse into the fears, the stereotypes, and moral issues that are dividing and confronting us today. (1995/2005 - 43/20 mins.)

Last Chance for Eden 1 is about nine women and men who spend two weekends together talking about racism. On camera for 24 hours, they struggle to find a way to understand each other's differences. In the second half, they ask each other questions they have always wanted answered. Their responses and reactions are compelling and revealing, but also intimate and honest. (2002 - 80 mins.)

Last Chance for Eden 2 is about nine women and men confronting the issues of sexism in their lives and relationships. The women discuss their experiences concerning safety, sexism, and sexual harassment in the workplace, as well as the role the media plays in perpetuating sexism and male privilege. (2003 - 69 mins.)

Last Chance for Eden 3 is for those of you who have viewed *Last Chance for Eden* Parts 1 &/or 2. This film is a perfect follow-up to the whole series. It focuses on the biographies of the cast members as they struggle to understand what had happened to them in their families and eventually, their journey towards finding healthy lives as adults. (2003 - 78 mins.)

DIVERSITY TRAINING MATERIALS

Book: *Let's Get Real*

This new book by Lee Mun Wah explores the questions people of color and whites are afraid to ask of each other and the answers that we are afraid to hear. Over 150 folks from all over the country participated in 'breaking the silence' about what separates and divides us as a nation, in our workplaces, and as friends. The goal of this book is to initiate an environment that will support an open, intimate, and honest dialogue for all of us regarding the issues of racism—what makes it safe or unsafe to share our truths, how denial erodes our willingness to trust, and the myriad of ways that we use to shield ourselves from being hurt or held accountable. (2011, 283 p.)

Book: *The Color of Fear: Twelve Years Later*

Have you ever wondered how the cast was chosen for this award-winning documentary? For the first time, in the book, *The Color of Fear: Twelve Years Later*, Lee Mun Wah, the director, will share how the cast was chosen, what it was like being on the Oprah Winfrey Show, and all the many experiences that occurred during the filming, as well as the original transcripts and pictures of the cast. As an added bonus, transcripts that have never been on film are included in this beautiful account of how the film came about. This book is a wonderful, behind the scenes view that will bring you to laughter and awe, at what came to be known as the defining icon for race relations and diversity conversations throughout the United States. (2007 - 100p.)

Booklet: *The Practice of Honoring Diversity*

Written by Lee Mun Wah, a community therapist and diversity trainer, *The Practice of Honoring Diversity* is a booklet of techniques for how to help agencies and companies integrate diversity into their meetings and institutions. Each of these practices were developed to encourage a more open dialogue where different groups could feel acknowledged, validated, and valued for their diverse cultural and gender perspectives. (1997 - 28 p.)

DVD/CD-Rom: Film Guides for *The Color of Fear-Part One* and *Last Chance for Eden-Part One*

The *Film Guides* were created by Lee Mun Wah and other diversity trainers to facilitate meaningful and insightful dialogues about our films. The films are separated into scenes which focus on specific cultural concepts. Available on DVD with corresponding sets of questions and exercises on CD, which can easily be printed for use with groups. *Available for **The Color of Fear-Part One** (1997 - 64 vignettes) & **Last Chance for Eden-Part One** (2002, 85 vignettes) only.*

Book: *The Art of Mindful Facilitation*

The Art of Mindful Facilitation was created by Lee Mun Wah to share his experiences and expertise with students, other diversity trainers, and anyone wishing to deepen their knowledge of race and group dynamics. The book describes his twenty years as a master diversity trainer and facilitator. He shares a variety of diversity experiences that actually occurred in his workshops, as well as his thoughts and the interventions he used to facilitate the issues that surfaced. Also, for the first time, he shares all of the diversity exercises that he has used in his seminars to stimulate authentic dialogues on race, gender, and sexism issues. (2005, 158 p.)

What Stands Between Us Racism Conversation Flashcards

So often we long to begin a conversation on race with someone who is different from ourselves, but hold back because we are fearful we might be rejected or say something inappropriate. Lee Mun Wah has collected over four hundred questions that People of Color and Euro Americans have always wanted to ask each other. A truly wonderful and educational opportunity for classrooms and groups who want to start a conversation on race, but don't know where to begin or what to ask. (*400 cards*)

The Point of Departure and Entrance

In every communication there is a point of entrance and a point of departure. Whenever I have noticed someone leaving a conversation (a point of departure) by reacting adversely to what another has said, very little is verbalized or acknowledged in the room that something significant has happened that has changed the dynamics between the person who is sharing and those who are listening.

The same is true when we sense a connection between two people. Though there is a physical, emotional, and sometimes spiritual bond that is observable, often there is little recognition that something significant has happened. Each are valuable learnings-entrances and departures – because they can bridge future communications or misunderstandings.

Mindful Facilitation is largely about noticing and sharing that something has occurred – a departure or entrance that affects the safety and intimacy of a relationship. Not acknowledging that something has occurred can create an atmosphere of fear and denial. The work of a facilitator is to help lift the veil of silence, and to notice not only what is said, but what is *not* being said. Martin Luther King once said, "It is not the words of my enemies that will be remembered, but the silence of my friends." Silence can be very deafening – and very painful.

What would it be like if we asked the speaker and/or listener, "What just happened here? Did you notice the impact of what you said?" Or if we asked the listeners in the room, "What did you notice just happened here? What was your reaction as you were listening? What's familiar about what happened?" Imagine the intimacy and dialogue that could come from such an "unveiling". This, to me, is what embracing diversity is all about – being honest, authentic and compassionate in our relationships with each other and with ourselves.

–Lee Mun Wah

"For change to be lasting, it must move the heart enough for one to act courageously – not just in a temporary sense – but as a conscious and purposeful act over a lifetime of different relationships and situations.

It is my belief that when we value others for their uniqueness and differences, then we enhance the possibilities for our children and ourselves. To me, that is what community is truly all about – when it is practiced and realized in our daily lives with those we love and with those we have been taught to fear."

~ Lee Mun Wah 2004